Murder by Wheelchair

ROSELLA RHINE

This is a work of fiction. All characters inhabiting this novel are figments of my imagination. Anyone who knows the Bay Area will recognize the setting of this book and will note any liberties I've taken with geography.

ISBN: 978-1-304-45069-2 (sc)
ISBN: 978-1-4834-0626-8 (e)

Library of Congress Control Number: 2013923232

Lulu Publishing Services rev. date: 1/17/2014

Chapter 1

I'd been a resident of Journey's End Retirement Home for less than a year when I found Mrs. Wilson's body on the Flower Promenade in early May. Ten minutes into my morning walk around the building, I stopped to admire the blooming rhododendrons recently planted by Mr. Kumoto, the Home's gardener, when I tripped on something protruding from the mass of bushes. Curious, I parted the dense foliage and saw the bloody mess that was once Mrs. Wilson's head jammed into the building's wall. Her body was slumped into the concrete like a Raggedy Ann doll, limp and lifeless.

At a place called Journey's End, it isn't unusual to find an obituary posted on the mailroom bulletin board at least once a week. The deceased's name would always be followed by "Passed peacefully in the Health Unit," or sometimes at a local hospital. But in the short time I had lived there, I hadn't heard of one found in a bed of rhododendrons.

Although I'd seen a dead body or two while working

for Sam Levine, a private eye in San Francisco, the sight of Mrs. Wilson shook me to the core. Even more disturbing was the deep gash on her head covered with coagulated blood, which had turned her tight white curls into a rust-colored Brillo pad.

She had recently acquired her new wheels after suffering a stroke, and was barely able to navigate the chair in her small apartment. So, why in the world would she venture to the Promenade without assistance? If she wanted fresh air, the Wheelchair Brigade (residents who volunteer to accompany wheelchair-bound residents for strolls) was always eager to help. More than likely, this independent, eighty-year-old, Southern lady would resist any form of help. "Y'all just wait," she'd say daily, "Dr. Hertz told me last week that very shortly I can get rid of this damn wheelchair and walk on my own two legs."

To be certain she was dead, and not simply taking a bloody nap, I felt her wrist for a pulse, and found none. Taking one last look at her lifeless body, I ran as fast as my aging legs would allow into the office of Dick Davis, the CEO of Journey's End.

As always, he was seated behind his oaken desk, facing the door. He had an ego as big as his girth, which explained the bookcase displaying several old sports awards he accumulated in his youth. And if they weren't enough to polish his self-image, the office walls displayed numerous photos showing him with various political figures, including senators, the present governor of California, even a faded photo of Richard Nixon.

He looked up from the *San Francisco Chronicle* crossword puzzle. "Good morning, Lily. What's on your mind today?" he asked warily.

I wasn't surprised at the sarcasm in his voice. Since becoming a resident of Journey's End, I'd taken advantage of his open-door policy by frequently dropping in with complaints about noise from neighbors in the apartment above mine, the monotony of the food, and a lack of laundry room availability. My most irking and constant bitch was the parking space assigned to me for Rosie, my newly purchased red Mini Cooper.

Every week, I barged into Davis's office demanding a new parking spot. "Am I doomed to that space forever because you think it's easy for me to maneuver a small car between garbage cans? Or do you simply have a bias against foreign automobiles?"

As a result of these many trips to his office, Mr. Davis and I were on a frosty first-name basis. Now, standing in his doorway, I couldn't help but think that in a few minutes Dicky would prefer a complaint about the parking space, noise, food, or laundry room to what I was about to drop in his obese lap. My ears filled with the sound of my heart pounding wildly, and my voice shook like a hundred-year-old woman.

"Dick, I hate to be the bearer of bad news, but Mrs. Wilson, the Southern lady from the second floor, is dead on the Promenade. I just found her wheelchair stuck in the middle of the rhododendron bushes with her head smashed like a dropped watermelon."

"Is this some clever way of getting my attention for another of your complaints?"

Geez, how arrogant could he be?

"I strongly suggest you come ASAP and look for yourself, Mr. Davis."

Like a child, he knew I meant business when I addressed him in a formal manner. So he put aside his puzzle and reached for the phone. "Please send Ms. Johnson up to the Promenade right away. I'm told Mrs. Wilson is dead in her wheelchair out there.

"Where? Oh, in the rhododendron bushes on the northwest corner."

Of course, he was duty-bound to call Ms. Johnson, head nurse of the Health Unit, and often referred to as Nurse Ratched by those of us who'd seen the movie *One Flew Over the Cuckoo's Nest*. Since moving to the Home, my biggest fear was someday ending up in her basement domain, sitting in a wheelchair, staring at the wall with drool sliding silently from my lips to my bosom.

"Lead the way," Dicky ordered.

As we walked through the lobby's double glass doors,

I had a sudden dread that perhaps I imagined seeing Mrs. Wilson's body. *Dear God, please let her still be in the rhododendrons, or I'll never hear the end of this. Davis will think I'm not just a complainer but growing senile. Out of spite, he'll send me to Ms. Johnson's domain in the basement, turning my worst nightmare into reality.*

We walked toward the northwest corner, and I breathed a sigh of relief when I saw the back of a wheelchair jutting out from the batch of colorful flowers, just as it had been earlier. Mrs. Wilson was still jammed into the stonewall; her head still showed a deep gash, and her soft, white hair still resembled a pot scrubber. For the first time, I noticed the copious amount of dried blood on the dirt beneath the chair.

Mr. Davis's face grew bright red, and because of his weight and stressful job, I worried he'd have a heart attack on the spot. A vision of him sharing a black body bag with Mrs. Wilson almost brought me to a fit of laughter.

The Health Unit was very efficient, particularly when a death was involved. So promptly after we arrived at Mrs. Wilson's side, Nurse Johnson came striding down the Promenade, carrying her black leather bag. An ongoing argument among bored residents was the contents of Nurse Ratched's tote. The bitchy among us swore it held her stash of drugs, while the more kindly insisted it was simply an accessory—like a Gucci handbag to go along with the white smock and stethoscope that snaked around her neck like a necklace.

After kneeling at Mrs. Wilson's side for a long time, Nurse Johnson stood up and announced, "There's no sense bringing her downstairs. She's been deceased for at least a couple of hours. Look at the rigor in her arms."

Neither Dicky nor I took her up on the offer; we simply nodded to indicate that she was, indeed, correct.

"I assume you will call the coroner and the sheriff's office, Mr. Davis. And until the authorities allow us to release the body, please keep everyone off the Promenade."

The calls were made from Dicky's office, while Nurse Johnson guarded the body and I stood a few feet away staring at the now-denuded bushes.

When the sheriff's deputy arrived, Dicky escorted him to the Promenade and executed his duties as CEO with great aplomb.

"She was found by another resident who was out for a walk about 9:15 this morning," he told Deputy O'Donnell. "Mrs. Wilson had a recent stroke, and our in-house doctor advised her to stay in her apartment with an aide, but she was a stubborn woman. I'm not surprised she didn't follow doctor's orders."

The sheriff's deputy examined the bloody scene, and wrote a report for the coroner's office, including a statement from me. When all the requirements were completed, Mrs.

Wilson was carried away in a body bag. It was incongruous that such a sad state of affairs should take place amid a plethora of blooming flowers on a beautiful spring day. Fruit trees and colorful plants lined the long, winding Promenade, twisting around the large, white structure sitting atop a very high hill. The building afforded each apartment a fantastic view of the indestructible mountains, and I found myself thinking: *Too bad we humans aren't as everlasting as mountains.*

Mrs. Wilson was taken down the back stairs to avoid the lobby, sparing the early lunch crowd the grisly sight. A dozen or so residents always met an hour or two before the dining room opened for lunch to talk, gossip, or compare notes about the problems of aging. Several of the women sat together daily anticipating their time and patience would be rewarded with a favorite round table in the corner of the large room. With walkers at the ready, they sat on benches, like birds perched on an overhead wire, staring at the dining room doors, willing them to open.

Today, however, word of Mrs. Wilson's death, particularly its manner, spread quickly, and the crowd was larger than usual. Someone pointed to me as the body finder, which led to a deluge of questions.

"How did you find her?"

"On my morning walk."

"Do you know why she was on the Promenade all alone?"

"I have no idea."

"Why did she end up in the bushes?"

"Mrs. Wilson had an accident in her wheelchair, somehow hit her head on the concrete wall and it killed her."

"Did you see blood, Lily?"

Disgusted with the insensitivity of this bunch of ghouls, I turned away, entered the elevator, punched the button for three, and walked the long hallway to my apartment. If today was my five minutes of fame at Journey's End, I could have lived without it.

Bad news traveled fast at the Home, often with grossly exaggerated details, so the top topic of discussion at breakfast, lunch and dinner was Mrs. Wilson's demise, usually ending with, "Thank God. It could have been me."

The next day, I was summoned to the Health Unit and the office of Nurse Johnson. "I have to do a written report, and I'd like to hear exactly what happened when you found the body."

How typical of this woman already referring to poor Mrs. Wilson as the 'body.'

I repeated my story, exactly as I told it to Dicky, fully aware that she'd check with him, anyway. Then, despite knowing I should stop while still ahead, I had to add, "Doesn't the manner of Mrs. Wilson death seem a little strange?"

"What do you mean by strange?"

"I'm simply saying she didn't die in a place or manner that most people go belly up around here."

Nurse Johnson gave me one of her Ratched looks and, without further discussion, dismissed me from her offices with a stern warning to watch how I referred to unfortunate residents who "pass on."

I had suspicions about Mrs. Wilson's demise from the minute I laid eyes on her body, but rationalized my thoughts as a result of working for twenty years under the tutelage of Sam Levine. He'd taught me well.

"Be suspicious of everything and everybody, Lily," he would tell me when we started a new case. "Don't take anything for granted."

Apparently, his advice turned me into a cynical old lady.

Chapter 2

Before moving to the Home, I'd been a happy, healthy, carefree, retired woman. After two disastrous marriages, I'd found the man of my dreams, only to lose him to cancer after fifteen years of wedded bliss. Devastated, I turned my grieving process into a nomadic life of travel and excitement—many visits to Italy, cruises to faraway places, weekends in Carmel, and trips to Hawaii.

But after a disastrous shipboard romance, I gave up traveling solo. I turned seventy and started looking down the road to old age. I told myself it was time to settle down and plan ahead, so instead of making plans for my next trip, I prepared for the possibility of spending my aging years alone. More frightening than living alone was the prospect of dying alone, with few friends or family at my bedside. I obsessed over obits in the daily paper that concluded, "She died peacefully at home surrounded by family." How would my death notice read? *Lily Lawrence was found dead in her bed by the SFPD after neighbors complained of an odor emanating from her home for the past two weeks.*

I would lie awake at night envisioning my rotting body smelling up the house, along with the corpse of my beloved Siamese cat decomposing by his food bowl in the kitchen. The gory images were enough to send me shopping for a haven where I would be surrounded by people.

I had my first look at what I thought would be my final resting place at an Open House for Journey's End Retirement Home. The apartment I selected was on the third floor, high enough to see the hills of Marin, with a lovely vineyard planted below to remind me of Italy's magnificent vistas.

But it wasn't long before I realized Journey's End was not Italy. Instead of a lilting "buon giorno" in the hallway, I was met with a feeble nod of the head or a cantankerous comment about the weather, the breakfast, or life in general. There wasn't a chance in hell I would ever be lonely, as people were everywhere in the Home—in hallways, the dining room, the lobby. I soon hated everything about the new life I'd chosen.

As an independent loner, I resented the communal meals, the various activities in which I had no interest, and the feeling of living at a kibbutz in Israel. But I put on a friendly face, always smiling, always rationalizing the reasons for my move. My only remaining hope was that someday, someone would hold my hand as I took my last breath.

The most joyous part of my day was the daily morning walk I took around the Promenade. I got up early to beat the crowd of other walkers, so I could hear the chirping of birds, see the blooming flowers and smell the fresh morning air in peaceful solitude. There was a sense of serenity on that long Promenade just beyond the hubbub of people. Until the morning I shared my walk, and the Promenade, with Mrs. Wilson.

Finding her body added a whole new aspect to my life at Journey's End. As a firm believer in karma, it occurred to me that by moving to the Home, I was meant to find Mrs. Wilson and destined to solve the mystery of her demise.

Chapter 3

A few weeks after the coroner declared Mrs. Wilson's smashed head a "Physician Certified Death," no autopsy was ordered and, according to her wishes, she was cremated. A month later, her family held a memorial at Journey's End. I don't know why death generated these occasions. Two hundred people crowded into the auditorium, and the event, called a celebration of her life, appeared to be only a means of indulging in good food and an open bar.

The Wilson family appeared satisfied that their mother probably became frustrated with being treated like an invalid, and, known for being an independent woman, had foolishly taken it upon herself to go for a ride on the Promenade alone.

The utterance of the day was, "Such a tragic accident!"

Her children said a few words, thanked everyone for coming and told how their mother was very happy sharing the last years of her life with the lovely people at Journey's

End. I couldn't help but think that I'd be happy here, too, if, like Mrs. Wilson, I owned a condo in San Francisco where I could escape on weekends to visit my favorite hair dresser, take in a symphony or opera, and dine in one of the city's finest restaurants.

Not that Shirley Wilson started life as a wealthy woman. Born and raised in a small town in North Carolina with six siblings, after graduating high school she was hired as secretary to the President of an insurance company in Raleigh. Within a year of her employment, she married her boss. Eventually, they moved the business and two children to California. Upon his death at an early age, she inherited a generous sum of money and a thriving insurance agency. Although lacking a college degree, she was a shrewd businesswoman, operated the agency well and sold it for a goodly sum upon her retirement. This elaborate memorial was most likely financed from the kids' inheritance, as they had spared no expense.

When the buffet and bar were finally depleted, people left for their apartments--most to take a short nap before dinner at six. All the residents dined with a group of friends night after night, a routine I found depressing and bleak. So I picked up my food in Tupperware containers every evening and took them to my apartment. I had no doubt my actions were a topic of conversation by the regulars in the dining room as they watched me fill the various plastic boxes.

"That Lily Lawrence is certainly a strange one," I could hear them saying. "So unfriendly."

Everything I did or, more likely, didn't do at Journey's End was viewed as anti-social in the eyes of the residents. Luckily, my newly adopted mantra, "Who gives a shit what others think?" served me well. Because most residents at Journey's End were aging conformists, I considered their opinion of my behavior, a lovely compliment.

I enjoyed eating dinner alone. After slipping into my fuzzy pink robe, drinking a glass of Pinot Grigio, and eating a micro-zapped dinner, I'd settle into my Lazy Boy chair and watch television reruns of *Law and Order, CSI* or *Criminal Minds*.

Mrs. Wilson's memorial was on a Monday, which at Journey's End was lecture night—something I never attended. Especially that night, when the guest speaker was Michael Hertz, M.D. His scheduled talk was on the causes, symptoms, and on-going research of Alzheimer's disease. I couldn't think of anything less appealing than listening to someone warn me that by age 75, I could be one of the 20% who might suffer from degeneration of neurons in the brain.

After my solo dinner, I had a sleepless night. A rerun on *Law and Order* stayed with me from the moment my head hit the pillow, and kept me awake for hours. The detectives on the series had a case initially determined to be of 'natural causes' but which ended up being a murder. Of course, the case was solved in sixty minutes, but for the life of me, I couldn't shake that show out of my mind. Considering Mrs. Wilson's strange means of death, and my proclivity for seeing the worst in any situation, I was convinced her manner of death wasn't all it was declared by the coroner's office—a sick lady's unfortunate accident.

Within the next month, there were two natural deaths at Journey's End—one from Parkinson's occurred in the Health Unit and a heart attack took place at a local hospital. Both deaths were followed by memorials in the auditorium, with more food and drink and, through it all, the loss of Mrs. Wilson was more or less forgotten.

In early summer, residents of the Home were invited to an annual barbeque at one of the area's state parks. It was a popular event that everyone attended, resulting in both of Journey's End buses being filled to capacity.

Before moving to the Home, I'd spent many glorious hours biking or hiking in the park chosen for the picnic, so I decided to attend. How could I not when the activity was to be held outside the walls of the Home, in fresh air, and at one of the county's most beautiful areas?

Just north of San Francisco's Golden Gate, the State Park had redwood groves, oak woodlands, and a spectacular view from a 2,571-foot peak. On a clear day, one could see the Farallon Islands twenty-five miles out to sea, the Marin

County hills, San Francisco Bay, the cities of the East bay, even Mount Diablo. More than fifty miles of trail filled the park and connected to a larger, two-hundred-mile long trail system. The twisting road to the top of the park's summit was a challenge to bicyclists and hikers.

As we boarded the bus, the day was crisp and clear, perfect weather for being outdoors. Our names were checked off an attendance sheet as we filled the seats for a short ride up the mountain. The Activities Director reserved the *Bootjack Picnic Area,* which had all the comforts of home--tables, stoves, barbeque pits, piped drinking water, and flush toilets. After arriving at the park, the buses unloaded and we made our way to tables covered in white tablecloths and fabric napkins. Small flower arrangements of tiny red roses completed the elegant picnic setting, and a trio of violin players was already playing their rendition of the oldies but goodies. A handsome young singer moved from table to table as he granted requests for favorite tunes from the 40's, 50's and 60's.

I found a table where some of my favorite people were seated—Roy, the Home's token gay, a couple of gals who'd served in the Peace Corps, and two staff members serving as chaperones. With delicious food in my stomach, nostalgic music filling my ears, and beautiful weather warming my bones, I found myself actually having fun.

After lunch, our little group decided to take a hike. The

chaperones claimed they would stay behind to clean up, so Roy, the Peace Corps gals and I started off at a pretty good clip. But a couple miles up the mountain, Roy plunked himself on a rock claiming he had all the exercise he needed for the day, and the Peace Corps ladies left for camp to take a pee. It occurred to me that when in Nairobi, they must have peed outdoors. Back in the States, their hygienic habits had, obviously, become more civilized.

Finding myself alone, I decided to walk another mile before turning back. The familiar paths took me to the top of a hill where I could see San Francisco in the middle of its beautiful Bay. Because most of my life-changing decisions had been rash and impulsive, it was no surprise to find myself pondering the question, "Wh*at in the world possessed me to leave that exciting city for a retirement home in the suburbs?* In my previous thirty-six moves when finding myself dissatisfied or unhappy, I walked away. Would I do the same at Journey's End?

Relaxed by the serene surroundings, I lost track of time and found myself with ten minutes to get to the bus. I raced down the hill, and, once again, my name was checked off a list as I boarded. But the bus wasn't in a hurry to go anywhere. Jack, the driver, stood outside with Neal, the HR Director, while the two mulled over the clipboard in Jack's hand.

There was an empty seat in the disabled section that

Mrs. Shaw, an elegant British woman, occupied on our ride up to the park. I assumed we were waiting for her wheelchair to appear before getting on our way. But a few minutes later, Jack raced toward the picnic area, while Neal headed in the direction of the trails. *Oh. Oh. Mrs. Shaw must be lost.* Since turning ninety, she was getting more forgetful every day.

As we waited, the grousing began.

"I need to go potty," Mrs. Nelson whispered to me from her seat behind mine.

"How about some AC? This bus is getting pretty damn hot and smelly," Mr. Alexander, one of the old curmudgeons, yelled out.

"We're going to miss dinner," elephant-sized Rudy whined as if he hadn't eaten in a week.

Forty-five minutes later, Neal and Jack returned to the bus.

Looking shaken, Jack stood by the front door and said, "Everyone listen. I have some terrible news. Neal just found Mrs. Shaw at the bottom of a trail. She must have wandered away, and, on the steep hill, it looks as if her wheelchair got caught on a rock and fell into the bottom of a waterfall. Mrs. Shaw looks badly hurt. We've called for a park ranger and an ambulance, so Neal will stay behind until help arrives.

"Now, let's all say a silent prayer for Mrs. Shaw, and we'll get on our way."

I'm not big on prayers, but, like everyone else at Journey's End, I loved Edna Shaw, who delighted us with stories of her childhood days in England during WWII. So I bowed my head and tried to remember the Hail Mary taught to me by the nuns many years ago.

The ride back to Journey's End was somber and quiet. In soft voices, people on the bus shared stories about Edna. How her husband brought her to the States after they met at an air base in London when she was in her twenties. How they settled in the Bay Area where both were professors at a local college. Childless, and with relatives in Great Britain, brave Mrs. Shaw moved herself into Journey's End Retirement Home after Mr. Shaw dropped dead of a heart attack ten years ago.

Until last year, she'd been an active resident: working in the lending library, knitting caps and gloves in the Knit and Purl Club for children in Africa, and taking part in plays that needed an actress with a legitimate English accent. But once she hit ninety, she became forgetful and uninterested in life.

As the bus rumbled down the mountain, an overwhelming feeling of dread and suspicion picked at my brain. Two bizarre deaths with wheelchairs were not a coincidence. Two unusual places to die were not a coincidence. Two frail, incapacitated women found dead under strange circumstances were not a coincidence. I could hear Sam's voice telling me, "Weird events are not a coincidence, Lily."

Could Mrs. Shaw's death be suicide? Admittedly, she hadn't been her bubbly self lately, but she was a strong woman who had been through worse events in life than turning ninety. I stared at her empty seat and pictured her slight, frail body on a gurney in the back of an ambulance on its way to the hospital, or, more likely, headed for the morgue. Although my gut told me these two unusual deaths were murder, the autopsy report on Mrs. Shaw again determined her demise was the result of "natural causes from a fall."

There was no memorial for Edna. Distant relatives on the outskirts of London decided to ship her body back to England after it was released by the coroner's office and declared an accidental death. It was rumored that the family was contemplating a lawsuit against the Home's staff for negligence. Inasmuch as Mr. Davis had a law degree in addition to his CEO duties, he wasn't concerned, secure in the belief he could win any lawsuit against Journey's End Retirement Home.

Other residents replaced Mrs. Shaw in the library, the knitting club and the players group. But while everyone settled into his or her everyday life style, I was a nervous wreck. I'd also become very unsure of the Home's sales brochure slogan, "Gain peace of mind at Journey's End."

Chapter 4

Obsessed with the manner in which these two women died, I was determined to call Sam for his assessment of my suspicions. I held back only because I had a sneaking suspicion that he'd think I'd become bored with retirement living and was looking for a job with him, or, worse, the Home had pushed me into senility.

"Get yourself busy with a hobby, Lily," I could hear him say. "And try to get out of that old people's place more often. From the day you told me your intention to move there, I knew it was a mistake."

I didn't want his comments about my chosen lifestyle, but my heart urged me to hear Sam say I was overreacting about these so-called accidents. Then, again, maybe he'd offer to look into my concerns. Since reaching sixty-five, he only worked a case or two a year. I was sure if he thought something was amiss, he'd be happy to get involved on a pro-bono basis.

In over twenty years of our working friendship, Sam always said I was the best assistant he ever had. "Your instincts are so good, Lily, you could open your own agency. Why don't you get licensed?"

I never had the money or ambition to go out on my own, but considering the latest events at Journey's End, it couldn't hurt to nose around, do a Google search, Facebook, use all those new social media sites now available for snooping. Maybe one would uncover a thread, which might unravel a clue.

While I stewed over Mrs. Wilson and Mrs. Shaw's deaths, life went on at Journey's End. After the picnic tragedy, the Activities Director scheduled the Annual Garden Tour and Tea. Held on the Promenade and in the lobby of the building, the event was a big deal for Mr. Kumoto and his son, Kai, who were responsible for the array of beautiful flowers and fruit trees. It also gave the resident nutritionist an opportunity to show off her pastry skills.

The itinerary was always the same. Mr. Kumoto led a tour along the Promenade, explaining the microclimates around the building, which affected the health of the flowering shrubs, perennials, and annuals. He had a gift for artistic combinations of color and form, as well as timing for the resulting foliage and blossoms throughout the year. However, this year there was a slight change in the tour. Mr.

Davis instructed Mr. Kumoto to by-pass the rhododendron area and concentrate on the Rose Garden.

Following the tour, a sit-down tea in the lobby included the nutritionist's high-fat, high-carb scones with jam, as well as brownies and petit fours. With my new attitude, I decided to attend.

All went well. Not one resident died on the Promenade or keeled over from the high-fat, high-carb goodies. Meanwhile, Dicky continued to assure us what a smart move we made by moving into the Home. Every morning at 10 a.m., the loudspeakers in our apartments bellowed out his daily announcements.

"Good morning, Residents. This is your CEO, Richard Davis. Once again, this is Richard Davis reminding you of today's event."

He then went into detail about the performance, lecture, or excursion planned for that particular date, and urged everyone to attend. Each day or evening, some activity was planned for residents, as the staff lived by the belief that a busy mind was an alert mind.

While the Home sat financially secure on top of the hill, the rest of the country was facing a monetary dilemma, particularly in the real estate market. People couldn't sell their huge houses for the prices they expected. In turn, they weren't willing to shell out big bucks for a retirement home. This led to many vacancies, making Dicky Davis and his CFO, Mr. Langley, very nervous. As a result, a new marketing campaign was launched, including an Open House with refreshments for potential residents to be held twice a month, and advertisements that aired on radio and ran in local newspapers, proclaiming Journey's End, "Retirement Living at its Finest."

The biggest change resulting from the strapped economy came about in the vetting process for potential residents. On my admittance, I was screened as if I was applying for a classified position with the CIA. Two health exams, one from my private doctor and one from their on-site physician, pronounced me in okay health. My financial accounts were inspected like an IRS audit, and, finally, after waiting many weeks, I was allowed to be an occupant. In retrospect, I wish the Admissions Committee had been a bit more perceptive about allowing Lily Lawrence into Journey's End. It would have saved me a lot of heartache.

With the lack of residents, and desperate for new ones, applicants had been admitted in the last few months with only a cursory look at their state of health, finances or backgrounds. As a result, a bevy of unremarkable tenants took up residency. Some were already in their 90's, on walkers or in wheelchairs. Many were single men who seemed to hold onto their independence longer than divorced or widowed women. In a place where the ratio of women to men was previously five to one, Journey's End became decidedly more co-ed, much to the delight of the single women.

Even I, who had sworn off men since the death of my last husband, was intrigued with the infusion of testosterone in the building. Actually, considering the men's ages and states of health, there wasn't a lot of testosterone, but the group of aging males made for an interesting scenario.

It wasn't the most appealing sight. Poor Kenny had all the signs of anorexia. Gaunt and string bean thin, he was a widower from the Midwest who moved to California to be near a daughter. And Elton shook so badly from Parkinson's that his soup always landed in his lap on its way to his mouth. Jack Marciano, a somber retired engineer, was healthier than the others, but had a creepy past. He talked incessantly about burying several former wives who died from a variety of cancers, and openly admitted to looking for a new Mrs. Marciano at Journey's End.

The new men joined the out-numbered group of long-time male residents already established in the community. There was Lloyd, who had never married, rarely spoke to anyone and appeared to be the youngest of this unappealing group. There were also the obnoxious old farts who ogled the widows, flirted with the wives, and imagined they were irresistible simply because they had a withered, idle penis.

When first arriving at the Home, I had asked Roy about

the single and youngest male resident. "You think this Lloyd guy is gay?" I queried him over a drink at the first Friday of the month cocktail party.

"No way. Why? You interested?"

"Absolutely not. I'm only curious because he doesn't talk to anyone, isn't as old or decrepit as the others, and he's never been married."

"Why do you women always think that because a guy hasn't married he must be gay? Maybe he has good reason to stay away from nosy women like you."

Thank God for Roy who I could always count on for an insult or a laugh. He had lived in the city most of his life, and his presence at Journey's End added a healthy dose of savoir-faire and sophistication where it was sorely lacking.

Summer, fall, and winter whizzed by without incident. The real estate market picked up, and so did the occupancy rate at Journey's End.

In my year of residency, I'd made no women friends until Monique Marquise arrived. A former dancer in France, she walked into a room like a spritz of Chanel #5. Her years of dancing had fashioned a woman with a lot of class and self-esteem. Because she never failed to wear a beautiful scarf around her neck, draped over a stylish outfit, she reminded me of Isadora Duncan. Not much older than I, she'd been in the US for many years.

Our physical attributes were vastly different. Short,

bottle blonde, and flat chested, I envied Monique's tall, stacked physique. Her long dark brown hair, always pulled into a bun at the nape of her neck, evoked the image of a dramatic accessory to an exquisite Armani creation. As an older woman, she maintained her knockout looks, which were exotic and sexy.

Although physically dissimilar, we enjoyed the same activities. Like getting out of the suburbs and driving into the city to enjoy an opera or ballet, taking in a foreign movie, or stopping at the lobby bar in the St. Francis Hotel before heading back to the Home.

One day, as we shared a rare lunch in the Journey's End dining room, I asked, "Do you ever question moving here?"

"Oh, I had no choice," she said. "I have very bad legs from my years of dancing, and am finding it harder to walk with every passing year. Sad to say, I will probably succumb to a wheelchair in the not too distant future, and, without family or children, this place will be a haven."

I don't know why the word "wheelchair" set the hair on my arms in motion. But it did. And in that moment, I knew if Monique were ever in a wheelchair, I would be my new best friend's bodyguard.

Chapter 5

I finally made the decision to call Sam, invite him to lunch and, after a decent amount of conversation, tell him about the two recent and unusual deaths at Journey's End.

He answered his cell phone on the first ring. "Sam, it's me, Lily."

"It's about time I heard from you, little lady. I was beginning to think you'd forgotten all about me now that you have an entire building of friends."

"Are you kidding? In the first place, no one could ever replace you. And, except for one lady who recently moved in, there isn't anyone here I would call a friend."

"I warned you that place was for old people, not a place for my Lily. But, of course, you wouldn't listen. So, besides being unhappy with your new abode, what the hell is going on?"

"I don't want to talk about it on the phone, so let's have lunch at Dolce Luna's where we can sit for a while and catch up. How about next Friday, or are you working on a hot case?"

"No case, hot or cold right now. Business has been so slow, I closed down the office for a couple of weeks and went to Mexico for a little R&R. Turned out to be Rosa and Raquel, which left me very little time for rest or relaxation."

"Good. Not about Rosa and Raquel, but that you aren't busy, because I may need your help on a couple of things that have happened here. So are you free for lunch? My treat."

"How can I say no to my Lily? Sure, next Friday is fine. What time shall we meet?"

After agreeing on twelve o'clock, I hung up, hoping I hadn't just made another impetuous move by dragging Sam into my delusions. I had a week to think it over, so maybe by the following Friday, lunch would consist of just two old friends having a normal conversation

It was selfish of me to drag Sam to lunch and pick his brain when I knew he was a lonely man craving scintillating companionship and conversation. He lost his wife, Rebecca, to a shooting when his home was invaded soon after he left the SFPD and opened his investigative business. The cops always thought the home invasion and Rebecca's killing had something to do with one of his slimy clients, and after a while the case went cold as far as the PD was concerned. The culprits were never found, but Sam never got over the event. The tragic loss of his wife is probably what made him such a great investigator for his clients.

He lived in a one-room apartment in a seedy neighborhood of the city, and one day I had the temerity to ask, "Sam, why do you live in such a dump? You can afford an apartment on Russian Hill."

"Because I won't find the scum who took away my wife in some snazzy apartment building. You don't understand, Lily. I have to live near the dregs of society. Being close to the pawnshops, I can drop in now and then and look at their latest acquisitions. Someday, these bastards are going to get rid of a hot item that came from the Levine house."

Meanwhile, I had some snooping to do on my own before meeting Sam. For the entire week, I sat at my computer and searched the Internet. I entered the names of men at Journey's End whom I thought capable of murder, starting with the long-time male residents and continuing with the newer move-ins.

I was convinced that a single man killed these women. At Journey's End, the married men were glued to their wives 24/7. They did everything together; ate meals, went on the Home's outings, participated in all the activities. I could never figure out how it was possible that after forty, fifty or sixty years of marriage, these couples still enjoyed each other's company. Some even held hands as they walked along the corridor. Most folks would find this devotion admirable and touching, but after being badly bruised in long-term relationships, I found it depressing. No, a married man would have to use his wife as his partner in crime, which (even with my imagination), I could never envision.

Of course, the killer might be some creep off the street who somehow got past the vigilant receptionist at the front desk, then killed Mrs. Wilson in her apartment and wheeled her to the Promenade. But how to explain Ms. Shaw's accident at the picnic? In order to attack her, he had to know the time and place of the outing. Besides, my instincts told me he lived on the premises. There was someone in the very place I lived who killed these old ladies for a very specific reason. I just had to find out who and why.

The new Resident Directory was recently delivered to my mailbox. With that in hand, I quickly ran through the names, crossing off those men who were physically or mentally disabled. If someone here was responsible for these dastardly deeds, he must have all his marbles to pull off two murders. He would also have to be strong enough to shove one hundred sixty pounds of Mrs. Wilson and her wheelchair into a wall, as well as push Ms. Shaw up a steep trail and toss her over. With these parameters in mind, I began to examine the male inmates who'd been around when these so-called "accidents" happened. It didn't take long to narrow my list of suspects down to a half dozen capable of committing a murder.

I immediately eliminated Bill, the shuffler, whom I met on my second day at the Home. Without being invited, he'd joined the table where I was lunching with several other women. Incapable of picking up his feet when he walked, his shuffling along the floor made him a target for ridicule. I initially felt sorry for the man, and tried to be cordial. But his action at lunch turned my sympathy to disgust when, midway through the meal, he shuffled out of his chair and in a loud voice announced, "Excuse me, ladies, I have to take a pee."

A week later, he called and asked me for a date. Horrified, I blurted out, "It will be a cold day in hell before you get a date with me."

If anyone would be a target for his wrath, I imagine it would be me. Luckily, considering his gait and urgent urinary needs, he didn't appear a likely suspect.

I continued to go through names of the men who lived at the Home when both accidents occurred, and came up with only six or seven. At least, my list of suspects was short. I spent a half-day going through names in the Directory, but without a hint of motive, it was a hopeless endeavor. Before spinning my wheels further and getting nowhere, I decided to throw the whole idea of murder out to Sam and get his professional input.

Chapter 6

As usual at noon, every table in the small Italian restaurant was occupied, including a table in the far corner of the room where I spotted Sam.

He was hard to miss with his mop of gray hair topped by an old-fashioned fedora, which he refused to throw away because he'd worn it at his wedding. Instead of a yarmulke, which he said is meant for bald men, he preferred the fedora to show off his hair, and continued to wear it for the last thirty years.

"Sam, fedoras have been out of style for decades, so toss it," I told him a million times.

"I'm going to be buried in this hat, so save your breath, Honey."

I finally gave up. For all the years I've known him, not a day went by that he didn't wear his beloved fedora (or one just like it) when venturing outside.

He stood to greet me as I neared the table and immediately doffed his hat.

"You look great with that dinosaur off your head," I said as we sat down.

"Still a nag, I see," he grinned.

"No. I just hate that stupid piece of felt glued to your head."

The waiter arrived, and discussion about Sam's headwear stopped as we studied the lengthy menu. Since I recently started a diet, I ordered the shrimp salad. Sam, who never worried about weight, asked for the house specialty—penne and meatballs.

"You on another diet? All these years later and you're still on a diet, even though you're skinnier than a straw?"

"Sam, you know how you're obsessed with the fedora? Well, that's the way I feel about my weight. So let's quit the bickering and get down to having a nice chat.

"How are you doing? Still in that fleabag you call home?"

"No, you will be surprised to know I'm moving up in the world and bought a place in Oakland."

"That is a surprise. When did this happen and why?"

"I finally gave up on the pawn shops in the Tenderloin and figured maybe the scum bags I've been looking for all these years are from across the Bay. I haven't closed escrow on the condo yet, but when I do, you'll have to come over and visit. The place is on Jack London Square, has a real bedroom and a view of the Bay."

"I'm really happy for you. Anything has to be better

than where you've been for too long. Maybe this means you're moving ahead in more ways than one."

"Don't count on it, Lily. Now, what's going on with you? You didn't invite me to lunch just to nag about my hat. And please don't tell me you've met some used-up coot at the Home and are getting married again."

"Actually, I do have some interest in the men at the Home, but it's not romantic. More like serial killer."

"Serial killer? What the hell are you talking about? You live in an old people's home. There's no such thing as murder where everyone dies from old age."

The waiter arrived with our glasses of Pinot Grigio, and I took two large gulps before starting my story. Gosh, it felt good to get the whole mess off my chest and share my suspicions. Being alone with these depressing thoughts had deprived me of sleep for many nights.

When I finished telling him of finding Mrs. Wilson on the Promenade and then Neal's discovery of Ms. Shaw in the park, my first glass of wine was consumed and I signaled the waiter for another.

"I know it sounds crazy, but both these women were in wheelchairs, unable to go far on their own. The coroner found no physical cause for death other than their age and the wounds suffered from these so-called accidents. Both were found in places way out of the ordinary, and neither woman was suicidal. So what else could it be but murder?"

Sam didn't say anything for a minute. He took a sip of wine, and buttered a hunk of Italian bread. "You know, I always said you had instincts like a bloodhound and, besides, you're a real yenta and have probably gotten worse now that you're an old yenta. But be logical, Lily, if something wasn't right wouldn't the big shots who run that place question these two deaths?"

"Are you kidding? Management would do anything to avoid scandal, even deny suspicious deaths. How could they call the place "retirement at its finest" if murders are taking place? Publicity like that would be a killer, excuse the pun, when they're trying to fill a lot of empty apartments. The downturn in the economy has had a huge impact on its vacancy rate. It's been so bad that for the past year, they're letting just about anyone who is still breathing into the place. Besides, the Shaw family is suing for dereliction of duty."

Sam was digging into his penne, and I knew better than to disturb his eating ritual. I picked at my salad and waited until he had used a piece of bread to wipe the last trace of marinara from the bowl.

"What do you think? Am I letting my imagination go wild, or am I just using my instincts the way you taught me for twenty years?"

He wiped his mouth of a drop of sauce on his lip. "Lily, if you feel something isn't kosher with the death of these two women, you're probably onto something. But, considering you have to live under the same roof as the probable murderer, I'd be discreet and careful about mentioning your suspicions to anyone there."

"Oh, I have no intention of letting anyone but you know how I feel about these deaths. But now that you agree something strange is going on, we can't let this psychopath get away with this or, worse yet, have him kill someone else."

"Whoa, girl. What do you mean we? First of all, I didn't say I totally agree with you, and secondly, if you're so convinced there have been two murders, why don't you call the local police and let them handle the matter?"

"With only my suspicions? No clues? No suspects? No reason to doubt they were accidents except for my gut feelings? Besides, the authorities and coroner have ruled them either accidents or natural deaths. If I said anything now, they would think I'm just a senile old lady with a vivid imagination. That's why I thought maybe you could help me out a little."

"Help you with what?"

"You have access to all the background tools the cops use, while all I have is the Internet and my suspicions. Maybe you could check out some of the men who live at Journey's End. The powers that run that place aren't especially vigorous in their vetting these days."

Sam shook his mop of gray hair and sighed. "Lily, I think your head and heart are in the right place but until you have more to go on, I can't afford to sacrifice my bank account and reputation chasing down someone who may not exist. Right now, do some digging on your own. Keep your antennae up when you're around some of the able-bodied men and get acquainted with them. Not too acquainted, mind you, just enough to find out more about their lives before they moved into that place called—oh hell, I can't even say its name.

"We'll stay in touch, and you can bring me up to speed on anything you find out or if anymore dead bodies turn up under suspicious circumstances."

I agreed to do some prying and keep him up-dated. He kissed me on the cheek as we parted outside the restaurant.

"Stay out of trouble, Lily, 'cause I love you like a big sister."

Chapter 7

I drove home, parked Rosie next to the garbage cans in the garage, and rode the elevator to my third floor apartment. When purchasing my unit the year before, I bought it for the view of the vineyard planted below my window, which reminded me of my yearlong stay in the Asti region of Italy. Now, I barely look at the vines, preferring to watch a vast amount of television reruns depicting various crimes.

My morning walk was still a must on my list of daily things to do, but with spring in the air, I started to take my strolls around the neighborhood. By summer, I was venturing down the hill, and walking to a huge mall where I could shop and mingle with ordinary folks. On the Fourth of July, an All American brunch was held in the dining room, complete with a chorus singing patriotic songs and food consisting of fried chicken, barbequed ribs, and a selection of sausages. Beer, wine and soft drinks were offered along with apple or cherry pie a la mode. With a menu like that, how could I pass on this particular event? Besides, it was our country's birthday party.

Following the meal, an old movie called *Yankee Doodle Dandy* was being shown in the auditorium, which prompted me to take an early walk. Heading down the hill, I saw Bob Wallace, who moved in about the same time as I, on his way up. I had never really met him, and we had never spoken, but what did Sam tell me? "When you're around able-bodied men, get acquainted with them."

Mr. Wallace looked pretty able-bodied as he practically jogged up the hill; so, as we passed, I said, "Hi! Do you take this walk very often?"

He looked at me oddly.

"Oh, I'm a resident of Journey's End, too." I said. "In fact, I think we moved in about the same time last year, but haven't had a chance to meet."

I put out my hand. "I'm Lily Lawrence."

"Pleased to meet you," he muttered, ignoring my outstretched hand.

"How do you like living at Journey's End?"

"It's fine for my needs."

I was getting nowhere fast.

"Where are you from?

"The East Coast."

Before I was able to ask more questions and get more curt answers, he was off like a gazelle and half way up the hill. I yelled after him, "Maybe we can take a walk together some time."

He pretended to not hear me. *You, Mr. Wallace, are a very rude man and are going to the top of my suspect list.*

Actually, Mr. Wallace was the only name on my list of suspicious men. I had eliminated Bill the shuffler; Jack Marciano, the three-time widower; and Kenny, the scarecrow. At a hundred pounds soaking wet, skinny Kenny wouldn't have the strength to push a stroller with a baby, let alone a wheelchair holding a grown woman.

I never considered Roy because he was such a gentle man. Besides, he didn't hate women. He just liked men better. And because he knew oddities about all the male residents, he once told me that Lloyd Bellingham was addicted to TV sports.

"Can you believe Lloyd spends most of his leisure time watching every sport ever televised on his 55" Sony? What a waste of time!"

With that information, I surmised the man probably didn't have any spare time to commit a murder.

I debated about Elton, a widower with prostate cancer. He had surgery and radiation treatment, both of which left him less of the man he'd once been. As a result, he had turned sullen and a bit of a curmudgeon. Could a loss of libido turn a man into a serial killer of helpless women?

Intellectually, I knew that was a stretch for motive,

but desperate and discouraged over wasting my time without a clue as to what I was doing, my imagination was working overtime. When Sam worked a case, he always had something--forensics, motive, sometimes even a suspect. And I had nothing except my gut feeling that a killer was getting away with murder.

That afternoon, I sat at my desk looking at names I hadn't yet searched, including Lloyd and the rude Mr. Wallace. I wouldn't be surprised if Wallace had never married. What woman would put up with this arrogant man?

And I figured the reason Lloyd Bellingham never married was his addiction to sports. Spending weekends and Monday nights in front of his big television screen watching the Giants, Forty Niners and every college football game played during the season, it would be impossible to find a woman who shared his fanatic love of even one sport. Tired and discouraged, I decided to get back to Lloyd and Mr. Wallace the following week.

Monique and I had tickets to see the musical *Lion King* in the City over the weekend, which would give me a break from thinking about murder and give her a respite from dwelling on the terrible leg pains she'd been suffering. She was talking about having surgery sooner rather than later, which upset me greatly.

"You've got to quit dwelling on negative events that may lay ahead and enjoy each day as it comes along," I told her daily.

How hypocritical to preach to Monique about taking each day as it comes, considering I spent a good deal of every day worrying about possible ominous events. If I followed my own advice, I would appreciate that there hadn't been another "accident" in months.

Following a glorious day at the theater, the following weekend Monique took to her bed, claiming she could barely walk. Within a month, she was in the hospital having surgery on both legs. Seven days later, she wheeled into Journey's End on a brand new scooter. I don't know who was more upset with the appliance—Monique or me. She assured me that the doctors said it might be for only a few months, but they couldn't guarantee the time frame until the healing process began.

"Now, you listen to me," I told her. "Don't go anywhere without me there to push you."

"Don't be silly, Lily. You don't have to push me. This chair is one of those new electric marvels, which doesn't take any pushing. Besides, how can you be with me all the time when you don't like going to the dining room for meals?"

"For you, I'll eat down there for a few months. It won't kill me."

The minute the word slipped from my mouth, I wanted to chew and swallow it up. "Kill" was not a word one used flippantly around these parts.

For three months, I faithfully followed Monique to the dining room each night at six, and ate whatever was served without a complaint. Meanwhile, I started to have what I thought were sympathy pains in my left foot. The foot had been sore since I slipped at the Mall several months before, but the pain had increased to the point I was barely able to walk. Not wanting to make a big deal out of a sore foot, compared to Monique's leg problems, I didn't mention it to her until she saw me limping to the dining room one night.

"What's wrong with your left foot?"

"It's nothing. Probably a little sprain when I slipped at the Mall a few months back. I went flying, twisted my leg, and landed on my ass. Boy, was that embarrassing."

"Maybe you should have it looked at by a doctor to make sure it's nothing serious."

"If it doesn't get better in a couple of weeks, I'll go to that podiatrist my mother saw every month to remove her corns and calluses."

After a month of walking on one foot, I called Dr. Falco. Being from the old school of medicine, he answered his own phone, and when I introduced myself as Nicki D'Amico's daughter, he became so excited I wondered if their long time doctor-patient relationship was based strictly on removal of calluses.

"I haven't seen that wonderful lady for a very long time and miss her smiling face. How is she doing?"

"She died five years ago."

"Oh, what a shame! I loved that woman. What happened?"

"She was eighty-eight, Doctor, lived a long, full life, and died in her sleep the day she was taking a bus to gamble up in Reno."

My mother had gone to Dr. Falco until her death, and thought he was the best podiatrist in the County, which was a generous compliment as she was very fussy about her feet. Actually, she was picky about every aspect of her life, which probably explained the dissatisfaction she had with my father.

After more chitchat about my mother, we finally got around to my need for an appointment.

"Corns and calluses like your mother?" he asked.

"No. I think maybe I sprained my foot after a fall, as it's been very sore."

"I think we'll need an x-ray. So come in tomorrow morning, and after the x-ray I'll be able to tell you what I can do."

Dr. Falco's practice obviously wasn't booming because he had the entire day open. I told him I would be in at eleven.

Chapter 8

Dr. Falco had aged since I'd taken my mother for her last visit. The tall, dark, handsome Italian was now grey-haired, baggy-eyed, and less attractive than the man my mother shamelessly flirted with on her monthly visits. But the twinkle in his big brown eyes hadn't disappeared, nor had his exuberance for taking care of feet.

After taking off my shoes, he took a look at the bone jutting from the side of my left foot and announced, "Uh, oh. I think this is more than a sprained ankle."

Ten minutes later, sitting on the examining table, he gave me the bad news.

"The x-ray shows a ruptured tendon, which almost always requires surgery. You also have an extra bone in each foot, probably hereditary."

"Surgery? I haven't had surgery since a tonsillectomy when I was five. And the only good thing I remember about that event was eating ice cream for weeks. I sure as hell don't think there's any tasty compensation for foot surgery. Can't we just wrap it up with an Ace bandage and let it heal on its own?"

"Ruptured tendons don't heal with a bandage, and you should get that extra bone removed, which will give you a bit of an arch in your foot. Get this taken care of now so you can walk like a normal person. It's not serious surgery, and you'll only be out of commission for a few months. I know a surgeon in San Francisco who takes care of the Warrior basketball team and the city's ballet company, so I know he'll do a wonderful job."

A doctor who cared for the feet of professional basketball players and graceful ballet dancers didn't lessen my fear of going under the knife, but I promised Dr. Falco I would call the great surgeon soon.

"Don't wait, as he's a busy man and it may be a few weeks before you can get in to see him."

That sounded fine with me, so after thanking Dr. Falco for the bad news, I returned home and put the business card of Dr. Keith Collins in the back of my desk drawer. But the pain wouldn't let me forget that surgery was in my future, and I could be disabled for several months. Thinking maybe crutches might be the answer to my future incapacity, I borrowed a pair from the Health Center and practiced using them around the apartment. Uncoordinated and clumsy, I couldn't balance myself on the damn things without toppling over. *Maybe I should use a walker or even, God Forbid, a wheelchair.*

I continued telling myself a ruptured tendon was minor surgery, and time off my feet would be a brief glitch in my normal activities. Besides, there hadn't been a wheelchair accident for almost six months, so I put aside suspicions about a serial killer in our midst and took up worrying about my foot.

Two weeks later, I was scheduled for surgery at one of the finest teaching hospitals in the city. And on an overcast, foggy morning, John, one of Journey's End drivers, drove me to the hospital. It was seven in the morning. The last thing I remembered before receiving general anesthetic was being wheeled into a large, cold, green room and lifted onto the operating table. I became relaxed and drowsy as sodium pentothal flowed into my arm, and fell asleep within a matter of seconds. Hours later, I awoke to find my left leg swathed in bandages and dangling like a side of beef from a hook in the ceiling.

Mercifully, just as with my tonsil removal, I was comforted with a special treat. Not soft ice cream in a little cardboard cup with a wooden spoon, but a liquid flowing from a needle, sending soothing messages to my brain. It was better than any cup of vanilla ice cream, and except for a wakeup call at six a.m. for temperature and pills, I found myself enjoying the peace and solitude of St. Mary's

Hospital. The nurses gave me more TLC than I received from my first two husbands, and although the food wasn't great, it beat the fare at Journey's End.

I stayed in the hospital for three days. The needle was removed from my arm, my leg was freed from the ceiling, and I was told I could go home. The afternoon of my release, I had the choice of leaving on crutches or in a wheelchair. Already aware of my lack of skill with crutches, and with one leg wrapped like King Tut in his tomb, I had no choice but to reluctantly accept the dreaded chair. I was not afraid for my safety, but I had developed an aversion, maybe even an obsession, with regard to wheelchairs. I tried to grin and bear it as John wheeled me into the lobby of Journey's End, where we took the elevator to my apartment.

It was early afternoon and I was eager to call Monique. Maybe she could come up and we could compare hospitals, doctors, and knockout drugs. My dinner was to be brought on a tray until I figured out a way to get to the dining room, but I wanted to talk with Monique first. Maybe we could wheel down to dinner together.

After trying to reach her by phone without an answer, I called Louise at the Reception Desk and asked if she'd seen Monique today.

"Oh, Lily, I hate to be the one to tell you this since you just returned home from the hospital, but Monique had an accident the day you left for surgery and is no longer with us."

My heart stopped. Tears trickled down my cheeks and I put a hand over my mouth to stop from screaming. *Oh, no. Not again. Not Monique.*

"What happened? Did she fall and hit her head?"

"No, her death was really quite unusual. When she didn't show up for dinner a couple nights ago, the security guard went to her apartment and found her strangled with one of those pretty scarfs she wore around her neck. It was the orange silk one, which apparently got caught in a wheel on her scooter. What a shame. She was such a classy lady."

With a shaky hand, I hung up the phone and sobbed for hours. Not only over the loss of my dearest friend, but the implications of her unusual death. Once again, the coroner ruled her death accidental and of natural causes. I knew better. Monique would never be so careless as to let her scarf get caught in the wheel of the scooter. And never the orange one from France. It was her favorite. The idea of an accident was sheer bullshit. Convinced Monique was another victim of the Journey's End serial killer, I vowed she would be his last.

But after placing a call to Sam's cell phone, I heard voice mail.

"Sorry I'm unavailable for two weeks. In Mexico for a

little R&R. Leave your name with phone number and I'll return your call upon my return home."

Holy shit! Was that man ever in the country when I needed him most?

Meanwhile, I spent many days and nights mourning Monique. One day, I asked the housekeeper cleaning out her apartment to look for an orange scarf.

"Si, Senora Lawrence. If I find it, what do you want me to do?"

"I want you to give it to me. Also, Martha, I was told to keep Ms. Monique's scooter in my storage bin until her relatives sell it. I'll get someone in Maintenance to bring it to the garage. And let's not tell anyone about the scarf or scooter. It will be our little secret."

For now, the housekeeper and I would be the only ones who knew I had the orange scarf or Monique's scooter in Storage Bin Ten above Rosie's parking space. Hopefully, one or both items might one day hold clues to her killer.

Chapter 9

My options for sleuthing were now severely limited. Fate had stepped in and confined me to, of all things, a wheelchair. Steering the damn thing wasn't much easier than hopping on crutches, because after a few rolls of the clumsy contraption, my arms grew tired, along with my frustration. Adding to my dilemma, dinner trays delivered to my apartment were discontinued after a week, leaving me to fend for myself.

Because of my anti-social behavior, I was hesitant to call on anyone I hadn't befriended, which was about every resident at Journey's End. Roy offered to help a few times, but the majority of his evenings were spent with friends in the city. Out of guilt or sympathy, my neighbor helped me downstairs once or twice, then forgot to call one night, leaving me to dine on a can of Campbell's tomato soup.

In the second week of my isolation, I answered the telephone and heard a man's voice on the other end. "Lily, this Lloyd Bellingham. I hope you don't take offense at my call, but I've been wondering if you need help getting to the dining room. If you like, I can wheel you down and we could eat together."

I couldn't believe my ears. Shy, quiet, Lloyd offering to escort me to dinner? Not only flattered, I was curious as to "Why." Was it out of sympathy, or had he been attracted to me all these months?

"Gosh, Lloyd, what a lovely offer. That would be great if you're sure it isn't too much trouble."

"Not at all. Football season is over, so I have no pressing need to eat in my apartment. Besides, it's probably time I got to know people around here."

That evening, Lloyd arrived at five thirty, ready to escort me to dinner. All eyes followed us to a table as we entered. What better grist for the rumor mill than for the two most anti-social residents appearing in the dining room as a couple?

Through dinner, I chattered about whatever entered my mind, eventually telling this strange man the story of my life. I can't abide stretches of quiet, and Lloyd didn't seem inclined to fill in the lapses. But he was a polite listener, even venturing a question or two.

"What sort of cases did your PI boss handle?"

"Anything that paid the bills."

"Criminal, divorce, civil?"

"All three and more because he sometimes worked with the SFPD."

"Is he still active?"

"Semi-retired. But enough about me. Tell me something about yourself. What did you do before coming to Journey's End?'

"I was in the financial business in San Diego for ten years, then moved to the Bay Area and opened an office in San Rafael as a Financial Advisor."

I wondered how he ever signed on clients with such a total lack of personality, but his sincere manner was probably a plus when it came to investing one's money. A number cruncher was definitely not my type, but if I wanted transportation to dinner, who was I to be picky?

Unfortunately, he was also lacking in physical appearance. Tall and slim were positives and in his favor, but there were a lot of negatives. His hair, like that of most men at Journey's End, consisted of a few wisps of gray over a pink scull. Deep wrinkles were etched in his face, and his teeth, small and yellow, looked like a box of Chiclets gum. *What the hell, I need a chauffeur, not George Clooney.*

"Are you from the Bay Area?" I asked, hoping to keep him talking.

"No. I was born in the Midwest and went to the University of Iowa. Joined the Navy and, after my discharge, went to

UC San Diego to earn an M.B.A. That's when I decided to stay in California."

"What do you think of Journey's End?"

"It's okay. I don't take part in many of their social events because I'm too busy volunteering with the Methodist Church, and the local hospital where I escort patients going into surgery. I spend about ten hours a week at both jobs, so it doesn't leave me a lot of time to do much socializing."

I was impressed. A man who volunteered at a church and a hospital? It was no wonder he'd taken pity on me and was so efficient on the wheelchair. When dinner was over, he wheeled me to my apartment and said he'd return the next evening. The stares and whispering diminished after a few nights when I explained to Roy, who had a knack for starting or squelching rumors, that the man was simply being kind in my time of need. Toward the end of the second week, I received another call from Lloyd.

Afraid he was going to renege on escort duties, I was shocked to hear, "I think you and I could use a break from the food in this place. Would you like to go out to a nice restaurant tomorrow night? It's Friday, which means poached tilapia or salmon, and, frankly, I'd prefer a juicy steak."

Holy shit! I hadn't been out to dinner since Monique and I ventured into the city several months ago, and the last time a man paid for my meal was sometime in the 80's.

I tried to keep the excitement out of my voice. "Are you sure you want to wheel an invalid into a nice restaurant?"

"You aren't an invalid. You're a lady who's had foot surgery and is disabled for a few weeks. So is that a yes?"

The next night, except for footwear, I wore my chicest clothes, put on my best face, and felt pretty damn good about how I looked when Lloyd rang the bell at six o'clock. We decided to act like people who lived in the real world and dine later than five-thirty, so Lloyd made reservations at a fancy place near the Bay for seven o'clock. We arrived early and while waiting for our table, Lloyd asked if I'd like something to drink.

"I'd love a glass of Sauvignon Blanc."

"Never heard of it, so why don't you tell the waiter, and I'll just have a beer since I don't know much about wines."

I was tempted to remind him that, like Dorothy, he wasn't in Kansas anymore, but I didn't want to hurt his feelings.

We sat in a booth overlooking the Bay, watching a full moon illuminate the water, while lights from sailboats cast shadows on the dark docks and a charcoal gray sky hinted at showers forecast for later that night. If it wasn't for my humongous appendage resting on the red vinyl seat, and Lloyd's lack of sophistication, I could almost imagine I was on a sexy date.

After eating the fare at Journey's End, the restaurant

food tasted like a recipe taken from Bon Appetite magazine. I ordered a plump, quartered chicken, served cold with mustard sauce, and Lloyd satisfied his urge for steak with a huge, blood red T-bone. Our voracious eating eliminated conversation, except for my interjections now and then of, "Wow, this is delicious." We shared a piece of cheesecake topped with dark chocolate for dessert, and after Lloyd paid the hefty bill, he pushed me out of the restaurant.

Clouds had formed in the dark sky and a dense fog, like cotton batting, covered the parking lot. Through the heavy mist, the ocean was now only a reverberating rumble of waves hitting the rocks on the shore.

We took a scenic drive back to the Home, and when Lloyd left me at my door, he said, "Tonight was a real treat away from this place. What do you say we do this every Friday night?"

Was he still being simply a Good Samaritan or was there more to this new friendship? At that particular moment, I didn't give a damn why he wanted to spend time with me. I just knew that the Home was suddenly a friendlier place and I was finally having fun. Who can say 'no' to an invitation that has a payoff like that?

Chapter 10

Sam returned from his trip to Mexico the following week, and I wasted little time in calling to inform him of Monique's death.

Between sobs, I blubbered, "She was my best friend. Actually my only friend here at the Home, and I really need your help in finding out who killed her."

"I'm sorry for your loss, Lily, but you may be jumping to conclusions because of your personal connection to Monique. How do you know someone killed her? The scarf could have caught in the wheels of her scooter by accident. Those new motorized chairs move pretty fast and maybe she hadn't gotten the hang of operating it."

"Oh, she knew how to operate it very well. I offered my help getting her to dinner, and she was adamant about driving to the dining room on her own. Besides, what about the other two strange deaths? You think they were all accidents, too?"

I was shouting into the phone like a crazy lady, and

the last thing I wanted Sam to think was that I'd become a hysterical woman.

"Calm down, Lily. If it will make you feel better, I'll start a little investigating with a couple of my contacts."

Following Monique's request, there was no memorial service, no obit in the paper, and no celebration of her life. And surprise, surprise, after examining her body, the coroner pronounced the death an accident due to strangulation. His report went on to say she died of a broken neck.

Her only relative, a cousin, Jacques, from France, came to the States to make arrangements for cremation and disposal of her ashes at sea. Before leaving for France, Jacques called to give me his phone number. "If you are ever in Paris, I would be honored to give you a tour of a beautiful city," he told me. "Monique spoke of you often, considering you a dear friend, almost a sister."

It was a lovely invitation but not one I was likely to enjoy. I was bereft with memories of Monique's wonderful charisma and the bizarre theatrical ending of her life. I had no interest in the life she had before our friendship, and was obsessed that her death was so similar to her idol, Isadora Duncan.

Sam got back to me the next day. "With all this talk about murders and serial killers yesterday, I forgot to ask about your foot. Are you still in the wheelchair?"

"No, but the doctor said I have to wear this ugly black boot on my leg for about a month. It runs from my foot to my knee and feels as if I'm dragging a boulder every time I take a step. At least it's a hell of a lot better than the chair, and I can get around by myself. Thank God I had a kind man pushing me to dinner while I was in the damn chair."

"What man?"

"A resident who offered to wheel me to the dining room when no one else around here seemed to care. Lately, he started taking me to dinner on Friday nights at some very nice restaurants. He said it's to get away from the monotony of the menu at the Home. What a blessing he's been."

"What do you know about this guy?"

"Not much. You know, the strong, silent type. He's probably one of the younger male residents, in his mid-seventies, single, never married. Roy assures me he isn't gay, although it doesn't matter because I'm not looking for romance. This is strictly a friend helping a friend. Besides, he's already in love with sports. I understand he has a gargantuan television where he watches every sporting event televised."

"What did he do before moving into the home? Those big television sets cost a pretty penny."

"He's retired from investment banking. Said he was a financial advisor in San Diego for ten years and moved up north to open a business in Marin. He's not at all attractive, but he's very kind and caring, which is what I need right now."

"Maybe I'd better check up on him. What's his name?"

"That really isn't necessary. He's just a sweet guy who doesn't have much savoir-faire and is sort of a nerd. The guy you should be looking into is named Robert Wallace. He's been a resident here since the year I arrived and is one of the rudest men I've ever run into."

"Being rude doesn't make a man a killer."

"Please just do some background on Robert Wallace. See if the SFPD has anything on him. He's probably from a large city like New York, Chicago, Philly. You know, a place where an arrogant guy might fit right in."

I heard Sam let out a huge sigh. "Take care of yourself and we'll stay in touch. Even though you're a pain the ass, Lily, I still love you like a big sister."

Meanwhile, Lloyd and I continued our Friday night dinners at various restaurants in the Bay Area. He bought a new Lexus and wanted to break it in, so one Friday afternoon we drove up to the Wine Country. I hoped we would come across a wine course on how to pronounce Sauvignon Blanc. It had become my favorite beverage, but when Lloyd ordered it at dinner, the name came out sounding like Swahili. It was such an embarrassment, I switched to Chardonnay because I knew he'd never conquer the pronunciation of Pinot Grigio, my other favorite wine.

The relationship with Lloyd was the most asexual I had ever experienced in my many years of dating. When I was finally able to walk on two feet, I would stand on my tiptoes as we said goodnight at the elevator and plant a little kiss on his cheek as I said, "Thank you for dinner."

But there was no affectionate gesture on his part—no handholding, no arm around my waist, not even a grab for my arm when I tripped on a curb one night. Roy continued to assure me Lloyd wasn't gay, but there was no doubt in my mind that the man had a problem relating to women. That was okay with me. I was perfectly satisfied with the status quo. A free meal each week at a nice restaurant kept me from dwelling on my hatred of Journey's End. To make matters worse, I now had an obligation to remain as a resident for the immediate future---finding Monique's killer.

Sam finally called to report in. "I've contacted an old friend at the SFPD and asked him about doing a background check on a Bob Wallace who might have come from the East Coast. I felt like an idiot feeding him such little info, but he was nice enough to not brush me off, and said he'd do the best he could with such little information. I'll call him back in a couple of weeks."

"Two weeks? Why can't you call him right away?"

"I'm going to Mexico again tomorrow and will probably be gone for at least ten days. Did I tell you I bought a little retirement shack near Baja last time I was there?

"Yeah, you forgot to tell me," I snapped. "Didn't you just buy a condo in Oakland?'

"Oh, this is just a get-away place for those times when I have the urge to leave town for some R&R."

"Is it Rosa, Raquel or both?"

"You don't have to be a smart-ass about it, but if you must know, Rosa and I have become pretty close these last few visits, and with my own place, I don't have to foot hotel bills."

I was furious Sam would put sex ahead of finding Monique's killer, but I stopped myself from saying something bitchy. After all, he was doing the investigating pro bono, and who was I to deprive him of some joy in his life? I would just have to plod away on my own until he got tired of the Baja trysts with Rosa.

"I'm happy you finally have someone to distract you from obsessing over Rebecca's killing, but I hope you don't stop looking for the scum bags responsible for her murder up here."

There was a long silence on the other end of the line. When he finally spoke, his entire demeanor had changed. He sounded like someone I just insulted.

"You know I will never forget what happened to my wife, and Rosa isn't going to distract me from anything. She isn't even someone I can talk with because she doesn't speak English. But she's hot in bed, and in case you've forgotten, Lily, a man has desires now and then. So quit acting like a yenta and stay out of my love life.

"If you're worried she'll distract me from helping find this so-called serial killer at the old people's home, don't get your panties in a knot. I'll call my friend at the SFPD as soon as I return to the States," he said before slamming down the phone.

Why couldn't I keep my mouth shut? By being demanding and pushy, I had probably put a horrible dent in one of the longest friendships I'd ever maintained.

Chapter 11

Eager to feel I was accomplishing something while Sam was off on his orgy with Rosa, I bought a stack of index cards on which to write everything I learned about every man I remotely considered a suspect. Then I visited Office Depot, purchased a bulletin board to hang above my computer, and pinned the cards to the corkboard. Maybe, if I were organized, everything would come together like a jigsaw puzzle.

The ugly cork bulletin board with its white 3x5 cards added nothing to my apartment's décor, but just looking at it made me feel as if I was accomplishing something. Because more action was required, I decided to look into Bob Wallace's background while waiting for Sam to report back. I desperately wanted him to be the bad guy, get convicted by a jury of his peers, and be carted off to San Quentin's Death Row where he would die with a needle in his arm.

I kept an eye on his activities as best I could. At dinner, I noticed he ate many nights with a group of six, including a very old, feeble man, a married couple and two widows, Ruth Stein and Olivia Moore. On a day I knew Ruth Stein was working in the Library, I checked out some books and gave her a big hello. She looked startled, as I had never spoken to her before.

"You're Ruth Stein, the poetry lady, aren't you?"

She blushed a little.

"In a manner of speaking. When I was studying the Freudian technique of psychiatry, I wrote a book of poems pertaining to the mind with references to the Ego, Id and Superego."

"Gosh, that's quite an accomplishment. May I ask you a big, personal favor?"

"I suppose."

I felt a little guilty telling a lie to this sweet lady, but rationalized it away by telling myself 'the end justified the means.'

"I'm taking a class on poetry at the community college, and have to write a paper on a renowned poet this week. Unlike you, I don't know a lot about poetry or poets and wondered if you could give me some ideas. Maybe we can have lunch tomorrow and talk about it."

It turned out she was more than willing, even flattered, that I would ask for her help, and the next day we sat across from each other in the Home's dining room at a table for two.

"I've selected Elizabeth Barrett Browning as the poet for my paper. Do you think she is a good choice?"

"Excellent, Lily. And I do know a lot about her, as I once wrote a paper on Miss Browning myself while in college."

After an hour of hearing everything ever written about or by Elizabeth Browning, I told Ruth I had plenty of information for my assignment and thanked her profusely.

"You have such a wealth of knowledge about poetry, I'll bet you entertain your dinner companions every night."

"Oh, I would never bore those lovely people with poetry. We talk about politics, world events, happenings here at Journey's End."

"They look like an interesting group of people, but I don't know much about any of them. For instance, the man named Bob Wallace. I don't think I've ever spoken to him."

"That's a shame as he's a fascinating man. He was born in Calgary, Canada and after moving to the States, became an orthopedic surgeon and practiced at a hospital in Southern California. His wife died about ten years ago, and he moved up here a year ago."

So much for his lie about coming from the East Coast. And an orthopedic surgeon? No way. I knew a lot of doctors lacked bedside manners, but Bob Wallace lacked civility. On the other hand, if he were truly a doctor, he would know exactly how to kill an old lady without arousing suspicion. And he'd certainly have the God-like arrogance to think he could get away with it, which would explain the finesse of the killings.

I finished my tea, thanked Ruth once again for sharing her vast knowledge about Elizabeth Browning, and told her we should do another lunch in the future.

Keyed up and needing time to think, I headed to the gym where I spent thirty minutes on the treadmill watching Dr. Phil on TV. The day's show was on the plight of battered women. Of course, there was a battered woman and her batterer sharing the stage, while Dr. Phil played referee, shrink, and judge. I hated these ego-bloated television personalities who exploited some poor soul's problems. Unfortunately, I had no choice but to watch the disaster on screen, because Ivy Russo, pedaling away on a bike, had beaten me to the remote. After thirty minutes of torture from the treadmill and Dr. Phil, I left for my apartment. It was time to work on my index cards.

I booted up my computer and searched Robert Wallace, M.D. on Google. There were hundreds of hits for the name, as I discovered three thousand two hundred men with the name Robert Wallace lived in the U.S. alone. Several M.D.'s appeared in the search—one with the Mayo Clinic, a plastic surgeon in Vermont, and a gynecologist in Oregon. None of the photos or ages matched the Robert Wallace at Journey's End. I also found a dentist and chiropractor, but all had wives, children or both.

After two hours of plowing through pictures and bios

for hundreds of men, I was about to give up for the day when I found Daniel Robert Wallace whose age was listed as seventy-two with a current address at Journey's End. After clicking on the name, a mug shot popped up. By removing the beard and handlebar mustache, the picture could easily pass for Robert Wallace.

The Google information indicated he'd been an attorney in Southern California before being arrested twice; once in January 2010 for driving without a license in Long Beach, CA, and again in March 2012 at Lake County, CA for a DUI. He was disbarred in 2010 for misrepresenting a client in Los Angeles, and moved to Northern California in January of 2012. Everything seemed to fit the obnoxious ass I'd met on the hill.

I was hoping Robert Wallace was an escaped felon or ax murderer, but at least I now knew he was a liar with an unsavory past. I didn't see a connection between his previous misdeeds and the three dead women at Journey's End. However, my discovery put Robert Wallace in a very bad light and proved what I suspected all along—the Admissions Committee was doing a second-rate job of vetting incoming residents.

I made notes on his index card, and pinned it on the bulletin board. When Sam returned from his love tryst in Mexico, I'd have him do a further investigation of Bob Wallace. Maybe he had other run-ins with the law I hadn't found. Maybe something like murder.

Chapter 12

The following week, I received a long, convoluted, mysterious e-mail from Sam.

"Lily," he wrote. *"You won't believe what I'm about to tell you because I can't believe it myself. I don't know if I mentioned I met Rosa in the Lizard Lounge, a bar on Rosarita Beach where I go all the time. The other night while waiting for her, I struck up a conversation with another gringo (can you believe there are about 13,000 of us down here?). He was pretty drunk and talkative, and when I asked where he was from, he told me Oakland, but was now living permanently in Baja. Said he had a problem in the States and was lying low for a while. Of course, I never let on that I was once in law enforcement or was a practicing P.I.*

"When I asked why he had to get out of

the States, he was pretty vague, just muttered something about a home invasion up north that went bad and he was afraid to get rid of the loot in California. That's about all he said before passing out, but I swear, Lily, I think this is the guy who invaded my house and killed Rebecca. He has to be running away from something more serious than a home invasion, and murder would be a damn good reason to go into hiding. I intend to find out where he lives, get him drunk and maybe get him talking some more.

"I'll probably stay here a little longer than I planned now that I've got this guy in my sights. Will give you a call when I know more.

I sat staring at Sam's e-mail. After reading it several more times to assure myself he wasn't pulling some stupid Levine stunt to get out of coming home, I had to admit he'd never make light of the worst event in his life. Maybe what he told me was karmic or some strange fluke, but it was hard to believe that his worst nightmare would turn up in a place he had finally found peace and romance. I hoped with all my heart that the gringo was one of the men he'd been searching for all these years, but I had my doubts.

Meanwhile, I pushed away my anxiety over Sam's lack of help with finding the killer at Journey's End. Maybe this weird twist of fate down in Baja was a sign I should give up my hunt for the serial killer and get help from someone in law enforcement.

With that decision in mind, I made the bold step of looking up the phone number for the county sheriff's office. After telling the operator the reason for my call, I was put on hold for ten minutes, until a deep baritone voice came on the line.

"Hello. My name is Deputy Thompson and I understand you want to report some suspicious deaths," he said rather matter-of-factly.

Oh god! What have I done? Put myself in the position of sounding like a crazy lady who will be the laughing stock of the entire Sheriff's Department?

Be assertive and sound confidant, Lily.

"I assure you, Deputy Thompson, I'm contacting you after much thought and deliberation, and swear this is not some crank call. My name is Lily Lawrence and I'm a resident at the Journey's End Retirement home here in town. You know the big white building on top of the hill?"

I imagined him picturing some senile, lonely old lady calling from Journey's End Continuing Care Unit where they kept residents whose brains have turned to oatmeal.

"I'm only seventy years old, in full capacity of my mind and body and, until my retirement five years ago, was assistant for twenty years to Sam Levine, the renowned private investigator in San Francisco. You've heard of him, I'm sure."

"Actually, Ms. Lawrence, I haven't, but please go on with whatever you have to report."

I took a deep breath, let it out to the count of ten, and began my saga of the three mysterious deaths at Journey's End within the last year. I started with finding Mrs. Wilson's smashed head on the Promenade, Mrs. Shaw's fall at the State Park, and my friend Monique's neck supposedly broken by a simple silk scarf. I held back on details for fear he'd tune out from boredom, so I gave him only the bare facts of each event.

When I finished my soliloquy, a long silence filled the other end of the line, and I was afraid he'd hung up after hearing of Mrs. Wilson in the rhododendron bushes.

"What does the management at Journey's End think about these deaths?" he finally asked.

Logical question. So how do I explain they abhor bad publicity?

"The coroner established they were all accidents, but I don't believe that is how these women died. My feelings tell me that the place, manner and means of death are very unusual for Journey's End, and Sam Levine once told me that my instincts are usually right."

Again, there was a long silence, and I wanted to bite my tongue for bringing up the word "feeling." Time and again, Sam warned me that the law dealt with solid facts, not feelings.

"Frankly, Ms. Lawrence, the Sheriff's Department almost always relies on the Medical Examiner's findings, but if you'd like to come in and give me some strong facts concerning these deaths, I'd be happy to speak with you."

I knew he was patronizing me. Granted, I had no facts to support my suspicions, but if we were face-to-face maybe I could convince him I wasn't an old lady with a big imagination.

"Just name a convenient time and I'll be there."

"How about next Friday around three o'clock, and if you'll give me your phone number, I'll call if I have to cancel."

Oh, oh. That didn't sound very positive, but I gave him my number and emphasized I'd be at his office next Friday at three p.m. I had huge fears of rejection, probably the result of disastrous love affairs, and felt he set a meeting date to get me off the phone. Next Friday, he'd probably call to say he was rushing to a bomb scare at a local school and had to cancel.

It would have been a hellish week to wait, except I had a Friday night dinner planned with Lloyd. A nice dinner in a lovely restaurant would help get my mind off next week's meeting.

On our way to Will's Grill in Sausalito, Lloyd suggested

we stop at a local men's store where he was picking up a new sport coat.

"It's been ready for two weeks after being altered," he told me. "I thought if we picked it up together, you might help me select a tie."

For some obscure reason, I found his suggestion the most intimate gesture he'd ever made. *Maybe he actually found me physically attractive, but from lack of practice, rather than desire, doesn't know how to display it.*

I was in an up-beat mood, the best I'd been since being freed of the big black boot on my left foot. With an appointment to talk with a real-life authority figure that might actually investigate the murders, and Lloyd wanting my help with his wardrobe, I was ready to party.

Upon being seated at the restaurant, I told the waiter, "I'd like a Stoli vodka on the rocks with a slice of lemon. Oh, and a bottle of Sauvignon Blanc."

Lloyd looked at me in surprise. "I didn't know you drank hard liquor."

Because the Chardonnay could never live up to my affection for Sauvignon Blanc, I rarely had more than one glass of wine with dinner. But this was a night for relaxation and celebration in anticipation of my upcoming appointment with Deputy Thompson.

The restaurant proved to be a winner. I sipped my vodka while waiting for dinner, which I proceeded to wolf down, along with several glasses of the fine wine. It flowed down my throat like a parched camel on the desert, and by the time we left the restaurant, I was more than a little drunk.

"I don't remember ever seeing you consume the amount of liquor you drank tonight," Lloyd commented on our drive home. "Celebrating something?"

"Only the fact I'm finally getting someone in authority to listen to my suspicions about strange happenings at the Home."

Oops. As usual, the copious amount of liquor had loosened my tongue.

"What strange happenings?"

Sam advised me not to tell anyone of my suspicions. But Lloyd wasn't just anyone. He'd let me pick out his tie tonight, said I had good taste and, more importantly, helped me escape the Home every Friday night for many months. He'd been a good friend and now that Monique was gone my only confidant at Journey's End.

"It's kind of a long story, so why don't we stop at your apartment, which I've never seen, have a glass of wine, and I'll tell you my theory."

Although surprised, he was amenable to my suggestion. After parking the Lexus, we entered the elevator where he pushed the number four, taking us to his penthouse apartment. At 1400 square feet, it was enormous compared to my minuscule space. It had three bedrooms, two baths, as well as a huge outside deck with breathtaking views.

The décor was surprisingly impeccable. One look and I was convinced it was put together with the help of a professional decorator. A white sofa strewn with dark blue pillows faced the brick fireplace, topped by his fifty-five-inch television. The rich dark wood of the dining room table and chairs added warmth, and tasteful blue accessories, placed in strategic spots, gave the room a special charm.

When he went to the kitchen for wine glasses, I peeked in the master bedroom. A king size bed was covered with a navy blue comforter and a small pale blue sofa with toss pillows nestled under the room's bay window. No doubt he liked blue, and definitely paid someone to design this place. No man, with the exception of Roy, could get this place so well coordinated. Besides, as I discovered earlier this evening, he couldn't select a tie without help.

Returning to the living room with two glasses of wine, Lloyd sat on a leather recliner. I sat across the room on his large white sofa. The seating arrangement was obvious avoidance of close contact and confused the hell out of me. At that moment, I made up my mind to discover the man's true sexual orientation before the night was over.

This last glass of wine might just give me the courage to try something outrageous.

But the glass slipped from my hand on its way to my lips. Wine splattered everywhere. The pristine white sofa, toss pillows; even the glass-topped coffee table shimmered in drops of the tasty liquid. Lloyd leapt from his recliner, raced to the kitchen, and grabbed a handful of paper towels.

I sat dumbfounded and humiliated by my clumsiness.

"I'm so sorry, Lloyd. If it's any comfort, it wasn't red wine. I wonder if white wine stains. If so, please let me pay for any cleaning."

"Don't worry, Lily," he said sponging off the couch, pillows and coffee table.

"My decorator told me this fabric was treated with Scotch Guard to prevent staining and…."

"I know the purpose of Scotch Guard," I snapped.

What the hell? Did he think I knew as little about cleaning products as he knew about wines?

After wiping up the mess, he sat back on the recliner. He was quieter than usual and my clumsiness cast a pall in the room. After a pretty nice evening, I'd ruined it because of my less than sober state.

"Well, guess I've done enough damage for the night. It's probably time for me to head home."

"Don't go yet. I want to hear more about those suspicions you mentioned earlier. Sounds intriguing."

"Maybe later. I'm going to have a huge hangover

tomorrow, so I'd better get home, take a couple aspirin and hit the sack."

But before heading for the front door, I walked to the recliner, bent down, and planted a long, wet, open-mouthed kiss on his lips.

"Thanks for a lovely dinner," I whispered over his heavy breathing.

Closing the door behind me, I entered the elevator satisfied the man wasn't a complete eunuch.

Chapter 13

The following week dragged along. I went to my Book Club on Tuesday and my volunteer job at the American Cancer Society on Thursday morning. Friday, I awoke at the crack of dawn, showered and shampooed my hair. There was a touch of autumn in the air, so I selected my wardrobe for the cool weather—black wool slacks, white sweater and a black leather jacket. I hoped the leather jacket would convey a hip, young image.

Although I didn't expect to hear from Lloyd after ruining his couch and sexually assaulting him the previous week, he called on Thursday to confirm our Friday night date.

"Can we make it for around six-thirty?" I asked. "I'm meeting someone at three tomorrow afternoon and don't know how long I'll be."

I wanted to have enough time after meeting with Deputy Thompson to mull over its outcome.

"No problem. Maybe we can go to the restaurant where

we ate last week. I thought it was excellent, and you seemed to enjoy it."

I couldn't tell if he was referring to my getting hammered, the French kiss, or was simply being polite.

"Yea, that's fine. See you around six?"

Although the Sheriff's Department was a ten-minute ride from the Home, I left for the Civic Center at two-thirty to assure a parking spot near Thompson's office in the huge county building. If a great parking space was a good omen, our meeting should yield very positive results. I found a spot for Rosie directly at the entrance to the building. It took me ten minutes to walk miles of corridors before finding the deputy's office, yet I was still early. The receptionist at the front counter told me to take a seat.

"I'll tell Deputy Thompson you've arrived," she said smiling.

My paranoia set in. Had the deputy forewarned her that a crackpot from an old people's home was coming in to report serial murders?

At five minutes after three, a tall burly black man appeared from behind the counter with his hand outstretched. "Ms. Lawrence, I presume?"

He had to be over six feet tall and at least two hundred pounds of muscle, leaving me even more intimidated. We shook hands and he led me to his private office down another long hallway. Opening the door with his name printed in gold, he said,

"Go in and have a seat. Can I get you something to drink? Coffee, tea, water?"

"No thanks. I'm fine," I mumbled as he walked away. A few minutes later he returned holding a paper cup with a tea bag hanging over its edge.

After settling behind his desk he said, "Frankly, Ms. Lawrence, the little bit you related on the phone, piqued my interest. I know someone with parents living at Journey's End, and from what I've heard, it doesn't appear to be a place where murder, let alone three murders, would ever take place."

"And that is exactly why I think these events are murder. Deaths are common up there, but not in the manner these three occurred."

He sat back in his big, black leather chair, placed his big, black hands on the big, black desk and said, "Okay. Tell me everything you know about these events."

For the next two hours, I did exactly that, starting with my discovery of Mrs. Wilson on the Promenade, Mrs. Shaw's fall at the park, and, finally, the sad, weird 'accident,' which caused the death of my friend, Monique.

"All three events seemed well-planned. They were committed without forensics of any kind, and the bodies were left in places where they would be easily found. Whoever committed these murders had to be a resident of Journey's End in order to pull them off so that they would look like accidents. And he did it without fear of discovery."

Deputy Thompson listened intently. "I can see why you might be suspicious," he finally said. "But without any evidence, motive or connection between these three ladies, other than they all lived at Journey's End, it's difficult to make a case for murder. All I can suggest for now, Ms. Lawrence, is to find some sort of evidence that ties these deaths together. If you do, call me and we'll talk again."

I left the Sheriff's Department feeling more dejected than when I arrived. I seemed to be the only one who wanted justice for these ladies. But I had to keep trying. Maybe I could find DMV records or employment histories on the Internet. It sure would help if Sam were home to help me out. Maybe I could talk him into working online down in Baja. If someone had a history of arrests, even a goddamn speeding ticket, Deputy Thompson might be willing to do some investigating.

The day was beautiful, so I decided to take a drive to the beach. Maybe the salt air would clear my head and calm me down. I drove the winding road around bucolic farms where sheep, cows, and horses stood in green fields, heads bowed eating a late lunch or early dinner from the grassy fields.

After parking behind a seawall, I took a deep breath before heading for the beach. I wanted a sense of serenity and peace after my afternoon with Deputy Thompson. Stepping onto the warm pavement, I smelled a potpourri of scents and was struck by the profound differences: clean, crisp salt air, rotting fish carcasses, tempting aromas emanating from a nearby barbeque stand. The various smells clouded my senses.

Since the killings at Journey's End, my wonder at the foibles of mankind had been heightened as never before. Chalk it up to aging or the wisdom and insight that accompany the senior years, but I had begun to question my every opinion about the people around me. Could one man's quirks make him suspect in a crime, and the goodness in another brand him as innocent? A combination of good and evil must exist in everyone—especially a killer. Heck, Robert Louis Stevenson had that figured out decades ago when he wrote about Dr. Jekyll and Mr. Hyde.

I had been looking for the most likely culprit, instead of looking at those less capable. I'd eliminated the week, frail, nasty old men. Maybe I should start looking into those I decided were incapable. Given the right circumstances, everyone has a propensity for evil.

Chapter 14

I arrived home a couple hours before Lloyd was to pick me up for our dinner date. After squeezing Rosie between the garbage bins, I entered the elevator and pushed number one for the Promenade. The meeting with Deputy Thompson, and its lack of results, had turned into a huge disappointment. Just as Sam told me weeks ago, "Law enforcement isn't going to waste their meager resources on suspicions that a crime has been committed without evidence to back it up."

Wandering down the Promenade to the spot where I'd discovered Mrs. Wilson's body months before, I headed straight for the bushes where her wheelchair was crushed into the wall. At the time, no one looked for evidence because her death was considered an accident. Maybe I'd get lucky and find something—anything—that would confirm my suspicions.

In an attempt to keep my spiffy attire from getting dirty, I pushed the leaves aside and peered at the ground below.

The pink flowers were gone but the greenery remained. Dicky had instructed Mr. Kumoto to put this portion of the garden low on his priority list for upkeep.

Luckily, the ground was dry from lack of rain, and I was able to step into the bushes without ruining my shoes. If there were footprints, they were long gone and, of course, Mrs. Wilson's blood had been wiped off the wall immediately after removal of her body. I hoped no one saw me scavenging around in the dirt. Besides, what in the world was I looking for? Stepping away, I gave one last cursory look and thought I saw a thin white filament, hanging from a back branch. I moved back, thinking it was a worm or some other creepy creature. But after seeing that it hung steadily and didn't wiggle, I lifted the small thread from the branch. Holding it between my thumb and forefinger, I felt its smooth texture, as soft and fine as an alpaca or cashmere thread. Maybe from a cashmere sweater?

My heart raced with excitement. Intellectually, I knew it could have come from anything or anybody, although it was unlikely. Mr. Kumoto hadn't tended this portion of the garden since Mrs. Wilson's death, and I doubted he wore expensive wool sweaters when digging in the garden. The only other person in these bushes in recent months was Mrs. Wilson, and she was clad in a blue silk robe.

I doubted if Nurse Ratched owned anything cashmere.

She'd never been seen in anything other than her green nylon smock. And by the time the Coroner arrived, Nurse Ratched had pulled the wheelchair onto the pavement, which told me that this sliver of thread had been caught on the bushes when the killer pushed Mrs. Wilson into the wall. Although not much to go on, it was my first tangible clue. Now, all I had to do was look for a well-dressed man wearing a white cashmere sweater.

At six-thirty on the dot, Lloyd rang my doorbell. After finding my first possible clue, I wanted to stay home and play around with ideas as to how it got caught in the bushes. But with Lloyd standing at the door holding a bunch of my favorite yellow roses, what could I say to cancel our date?

Without consulting me, he changed his mind about the restaurant. "I found another new spot in Sausalito, which claims to serve the finest sushi in the county."

Too bad he hadn't checked with me first, as I'm not a big fan of raw fish. In retrospect, I should have reneged on this dinner, but I faked my way through the evening by nibbling on several selections from the menu.

"You're not eating much tonight, Lily. Feeling okay?"

"I have a slight headache and, truthfully, I'm not crazy about sushi."

"Sorry, I should have asked. With your wine sophistication, I assumed you enjoyed exotic foods."

Was that a sarcastic jab? And was the restaurant selection

revenge for soiling his sofa and disturbing his libido the previous week? But the sake had mellowed me out, so I ignored his comment and decided to enjoy the evening.

With dinner over, Lloyd put his credit card on the table and signaled the waiter for the check. We had almost reached the Home when Lloyd surprised me by saying, "By the way, Lily, you started to tell me something last week about strange happenings at Journey's End, but never finished the story."

Damn. I thought the kiss in his apartment had traumatized him to the point he'd forgotten my comment. Since I wasn't quick on my feet when it came to lying, I had no idea what I could concoct to satisfy his curiosity. *How about a fake rumor at the Home? That was certainly a likely event.*

"I'm surprised you didn't hear the gossip, because it turned out to be one of the best stories ever concocted at Journey's End. Seems as if someone saw a man in a white uniform sneaking out of Muriel Brown's apartment at one o'clock in the morning the past few weeks. Of course, the rumor mill went wild. Everyone decided the culprit was Joe Borelli, that guard who once danced professionally. With his sexy mustache and muscular body, he's pretty good-looking, so it was inevitable he'd be pegged right away.

"Then Muriel heard the rumor and squelched it ASAP. She assured everyone it was a terrible lie, saving Joe from losing his reputation and job. Apparently, the story was started by one of his co-workers who had a grudge against Borelli, and was trying to get his ass canned. Can you believe someone would do something like that?"

I felt bad implicating an innocent security guard in my lie, but it was the best I could concoct on short notice. Lloyd appeared to accept my story because it wasn't unusual for outlandish rumors to fly around the Home, especially those dealing with sexual overtones.

Thank God, the uncomfortable events of the previous Friday evening, particularly the half-second when my tongue was down his throat, occurred in the privacy of his apartment. There could never be rumors circulating about that true sexy event unless Lloyd or I announced it over the CEO's loudspeaker. And there was fat chance of that ever happening. It was also a safe bet neither of us would speak to the other of that night in the future. However, I had to inquire about the sofa.

"Were you able to remove the wine from that pretty white couch?"

I snuck a quick peek at his face and could swear it turned a deep crimson red. Was the mere thought of that evening enough to shake up whatever was in his strange psyche? He waited until we were in the garage before answering, "It's good as new. One would never know anything was spilled."

"I'm glad to hear that. Next time you invite me to your apartment, I promise to behave."

Then remembering I did the inviting and not Lloyd, I doubted there would be a next time at his apartment, so I invited him to mine.

"Would you like to come to my place Sunday night for dinner? I'll cook us a homemade meal. Consider it a small repayment for all the lovely dinners you've bought me."

He seemed genuinely pleased with my offer. "Come down about 5:30, and we can have a cocktail first."

Chapter 15

After extending the dinner invitation, I had second thoughts. I wasn't much of a cook in the first place, and I now had to plan a menu and shop for a bottle of bourbon. The next morning, I looked up 'easy recipes' on the computer, found a chicken casserole that looked more elegant than it sounded, and wrote out a shopping list.

Late in the day, I checked my e-mail and found one from Sam sent the night before.

> *"Lily, I was going to call but figured e-mail was cheaper and more reliable than the phone service down here. First of all, you won't believe my unexpected luck in meeting that gringo at the Lizard Lounge. Mexico must have something to do with my good fortune—first, Rosa and then this Jose fellow. For a so-called great*

investigator, I was sure doing a shitty job all those years looking in the wrong places.

"After getting him drunk as a skunk on tequila last night at the shack where he lives near the beach, he told me his name is Jose Hernandez and is originally from some small town outside Mexico City. He got to the States illegally through the Arizona border way back in the 80's, and lived up and down the California coast picking fruit for twenty years. He got into a life of crime a few years back when he hooked up with another picker in the Central Valley, who he said was named Pablo Gutierrez. (Actually, he didn't say 'life of crime'. He said 'another profession.') They started using drugs and when they ran out of money to pay for their fix, they moved on to whatever crime could pay for their habit—purse snatching, identity theft, and, recently, home invasions.

"Honest to God, Lily, when I heard that, every nerve in my body started shaking like those silly Mexican jumping beans. He told me they'd break into houses when people were at work and take whatever they could pawn or sell on E-bay. When he said, 'Everything was good,

man, until the last job in San Francisco,' I knew I had my man.

'We ran into some bad luck on the last job,' he told me, "when the lady of the house walked in on us. Then all of a sudden, my stupid friend goes berserk, pulls out his gun and shoots her in the head.'

"I wanted to put my hands around his neck until he stopped breathing, but I have to get proof it was my house and my wife Pablo shot before I can call in the Mexican authorities. Jose said he has one particular piece of loot he's trying to sell down here because it's a large gold candle stand, and he says the Mexican Catholics like to burn candles.

"I know it's the menorah Rebecca's mother gave us for a wedding gift, and if I can get my hands on that piece, it will be the proof I need to take action. I was about to tell him I'd be interested in buying it, but before I got the chance, he'd fallen asleep on the ratty mattress he calls a bed. Next time we're together, I'll make an issue of seeing his loot, and if he has the menorah from my house, it will be enough proof to bring this piece of shit to justice.

"Hope all goes well with you and your investigative work on the Home's serial killer. I promise when I've got this guy and his buddy, Pablo, in jail up in the States, I'll devote all my time to helping in your search. Meanwhile, take care of yourself.

"Love you, Big Sister".

Sam's e-mail was so promising and hopeful that a tiny bit of envy crept into my feelings of joy for his good fortune in finding Jose. The killing of Roberta had been an albatross around his neck far too long, and it looked as if he was now on his way to solving the most important case of his career. The fact that it was happening in such unexpected circumstances gave me hope that perhaps, one day, I would find the serial killer at Journey's End in some serendipitous manner.

Chapter 16

At 5:30 Sunday evening, Lloyd was at my door holding a bottle of Chardonnay in one hand and a bouquet of mixed flowers in the other. He actually looked sort of handsome, as if he had dressed especially for the occasion. The dark blue slacks, shiny black shoes, and white sweater over a light blue dress shirt were not the attire he wore on our Friday dinner dates. On those nights, he wore outdated suits from his working days, usually with some outlandish tie. I had to admit his lack of style was another turn-off, but on this night he looked as if he'd stepped out of GQ Magazine.

The chicken casserole turned out to be a big hit, and after a dessert of pear halves swimming in port wine, along with a biscotti cookie, we continued to sit at the table, sip Chardonnay, and discuss our diverse views on politics and religion.

Somehow, I ended up telling him silly stories of growing

up in a large Italian family, and how we kids always had a little glass of wine in lieu of milk with dinner.

"The best part of the wine was dunking my mother's home-baked biscotti cookies in it. She couldn't bake worth a damn, but those cookies became her specialty after a soak in my Dad's Chianti."

He looked bored to tears, but after a few glasses of wine with dinner, and the Sauvignon Blanc I'd sipped while cooking up the chicken casserole, I couldn't shut up. Besides, I didn't want to hear about Lloyd being nominated to serve on Journey's End Board of Directors.

When I heard the surprising news from Roy several days before, I was shocked. "Why would someone who hates this place as much as I do, and is less sociable than I am, be nominated for the Board? Other than the two of us, who knows anything about him?"

"As you're aware, Lily, there are few able-bodied people willing to serve. I suppose the Nominating Committee decided that he had all his marbles and a background in finance, which is a big part of the job when budget time rolls around. Besides, he was willing to run."

I was astounded he agreed to the nomination, and perturbed over losing a co-conspirator in my dislike of the Home. Of course, there was always the chance he wouldn't be elected so I forced myself to ignore the subject. Why spoil a night I'd spent a lot of time trying to make perfect?

"Did I tell you how nice you look tonight?" I asked him. "Your sweater is especially beautiful."

Leaning across the table, I felt a sleeve. "It's so soft it could be cashmere."

"It is. Cashmere sweaters are a weakness of mine. I have them in several colors, but this happens to be a favorite."

My heart quickened as I remembered the tiny bit of white wool plucked off the rhododendron leaves on the promenade. It was soft white wool, and I was certain the thread was cashmere from a sweater, like the one now in my apartment.

Be reasonable, Lily. Many residents own cashmere sweaters. I hadn't actually seen one on any man until tonight, and Lloyd never wore this or any other sweater on our Friday night dinner dates. Was I so desperate for a killer suspect I was allowing my imagination to run wild? Or was I simply pissed that Lloyd had betrayed me by accepting a nomination to the Board at the very place we both agreed to hate?

Wearing this particular outerwear to dinner had to be an innocent but very incriminating fluke.

At least that was what I told myself as I tidied the apartment before going to bed for another sleepless night.

Chapter 17

As the following Friday night approached, I cooked up a lie to avoid joining Lloyd for dinner. I needed time to mull over implications of the white cashmere sweater. I was about to call Sam about the latest development when, out of the blue, I received another e-mail from him.

> *"Just wanted to check in and bring you up-to-date on happenings down here in the land of sunshine, snorkeling, whale sharks and human sharks that come down here to hide from the law. Jose and I have become great drinking buddies, and I have no doubt he and Pablo are the two men I've been looking for all these years. Last time we were together, I had a recording device in my pocket and got him to tell me on tape that his loot was from a job they'd done in*

Frisco. Now, all I need is something tangible to tie him to the robbery at my house.

"Would you like to come down and join in the fun? You're probably ready to get away from that place you live, anyhow, and it's been too long since we've shared a beer together. There are some great hotels down here with spas, pools, fancy restaurants and shops, so you don't have to go near any of my tacky bars. San Jose del Cabo, a 10-minute drive from the airport, is a quaint shopping destination and if I remember correctly, that happens to be one of your favorite pastimes.

"It's only a little over a three hour flight from the Bay Area to San Jose del Cabo, and I can pick you up at the airport. Rates for hotels run from $500 a night at the snazzy Cabo Inn Hotel to $40 for a clean and funky budget option in the middle of town. (The price says it all). Just tell me what you want to pay and I'll reserve you a room for as long or short a time, as you like.

"Let me know as soon as possible because I don't know how long I can hold off confronting Jose."

I couldn't believe my good luck! Not only would a trip to Mexico be a perfect excuse to get away from the Home and Lloyd while I sorted out my thoughts, I really needed a vacation from Journey's End.

Without the slightest hesitation, I went on-line to Mexicana Airlines and booked an open ticket for the following Saturday. Not sure how long I would stay in Mexico; I was willing to pay extra money for a flexible return to Journey's End, Lloyd, and a serial killer.

I e-mailed Sam, told him to book me into a hotel with rates lower than $500 a night but more than the $40 he mentioned. I included my flight plans with arrival time, and told him how eager I was to see his smiling face.

> *"Meet me at 4 p.m., Gate Five, Mexicana Airlines next Saturday afternoon."*

Suddenly, the whole world looked brighter. I had something exciting to look forward to instead of an endless, frustrating search for a killer. More disturbing than my ongoing Internet search, was contemplating my next move with a man who suddenly was at the top of my killer radar. For the next week, I'd try to forget everything remotely connected to Journey's End and simply relax in the warmth of an old, trusted friend on the verge of nabbing his long-time nemesis. Hopefully, Sam's grand finale with the man responsible for his wife's death would end in his inimitable manner of closing cases—successfully and non-violently. What other outcome was possible in a land of endless beaches and eternally sunny skies?

Chapter 18

I spotted my old friend the moment I entered the small, busy airport. A straw fishing hat replaced the fedora, and his usually pale face was as brown as the natives who crowded around us. His body, now beefed up by tortillas, tacos, and tequila, sported a yellow cotton shirt, denim shorts and yellow rubber thongs. Sam's thin, stress-lined face was gone, replaced with a smiling, contented countenance. Amazing what a daily dose of good sex can do for a man!

We hugged and told each other it had been too long since our lunch at Dolce Luna's, then took the stairs down to Baggage. The 'aerodrome' was relatively small with only five terminals, and, of course, Mexicana Airlines was in Number Five. I could barely keep up with Sam's youthful stride.

"My god, Sam, you look and act ten years younger. I guess Cabo's R&R is exactly what you needed, not to mention the eerie coincidence of running into Jose Hernandez. I'm dying to hear how you plan on getting him back to the States."

My one packed bag was sitting alone next to the luggage carousal. Sam grabbed it and led me to the airport's parking lot, which was bigger than the airport. In a far corner, we stopped next to a beat-up version of a 1960's Dodge Dart. Its exterior was battleship gray primer. A quick look and I saw missing side view mirrors and a large dent in the left fender.

"It's better to drive a piece of shit like this down here than something new and shiny just asking to be ripped off," Sam told me.

He threw my bag into the back seat, and opened the passenger side door. "Step into my chariot, sweet lady, and I'll take you for a ride of incredible sights."

I'd done an Internet search for nearby Cabo San Lucas, which was a lot more fun than looking for creepy criminals, and found it was at the very southern tip of the Baja Peninsula. My search had dredged up a lot of interesting information.

Baja was once a base for private vessels waiting to pounce on Spanish treasure ships. Even fifteen years ago, it was little more than fishing and canning village, occasionally visited by adventurous sports fishermen. Since then, it had earned a reputation for the large marlin caught in the bay, which was now full of sleek, radar-equipped fishing yachts. Multi-million dollar second homes occupied the best vantage points, and with the golf courses and palm trees, it mimicked the Florida landscape. At first view it looked more like an enclave of the US than part of Mexico.

"Aside from the gringo who robbed your house who makes his home in Baja, is there a lot of crime here?" I asked Sam who was intent on giving me a tour of the classiest parts of town.

"Nah. Crime and bloodshed in some regions cost Mexico's tourist industry dearly. But the irony is, Lily, the country's tourist areas have always remained untouched by the violence. Traffic is easy to handle, and locals are friendly and eager to welcome dollar-laden tourists."

His comment reminded me of Rosa. I was curious about her relevance in his life, but I knew time and my prying mouth would eventually bring everything into the open during my short stay.

I gazed out the car window while Sam gave me a running commentary about the delights of Baja. From the car window, I saw playful sea lions frolicking off the coast, and many fishing and pleasure boats floating in the water. As we passed a crop of high-end resorts on the golden beaches, I said, "These hotels look beautiful, but way out of my budget. So where am I staying this week?'

"Yeah, these places start at about five hundred a night, so I found you a nice hotel with clean, modern rooms at a hundred a night and with a view of the water. Does that sound okay with you?'

"Sounds good as long as it doesn't have a guest list that includes cockroaches and bed bugs."

"It's a perfectly nice hotel, just not one of the snazzy places on the bluffs. Since you won't be staying at the very best, I plan on taking you to dinner tonight at the finest hotel in town. I've reserved a table at Las Ventanas al Paraiso, translated it means "windows to paradise." At least you'll get to see how the rich half live here in Baja."

True to his word, that evening as we savored roasted snapper and lobster with pasta from our open-air table, we could see the twinkling stars, and hear the waves insistently punishing the beach. After enough wine, I felt as if the sea was calling me, and, the next day that was exactly what happened.

Sam had arranged for a water taxi excursion from Medano Beach out to El Arco, the rock formation where the Sea of Cortez collides with the Pacific. Knowing I hated being on the water, he had to convince me of the trip's worthiness.

"We'll be on a glass-bottom boat with a view of sea life swimming below. And above, you'll see the most glorious rocks."

He was right. Everything about the water taxi excursion was exquisite, and, for a grand finale, our pilot dropped us off at a picturesque beach where we spent an hour walking on the golden sand. Strolling along, I had an urge to grill him about his plans for Jose's capture, but didn't want to spoil the peaceful day.

Thinking Rosa was a safe subject, I said, "Tell me about your lady friend. Will I get to meet her?"

"Of course, but I want you know there's nothing permanent between us. She's been an unbelievable fuck, but once Jose is in jail, I'm back to the States to watch him stand trial."

I breathed a sigh of relief and returned to watching sea lion pups frolic with the snorkelers, nibbling on food finds, and begging to have their tummies scratched.

Chapter 19

The hotel Sam booked for me turned out to be a pleasant surprise, with a price tag of only a hundred dollars per night, plus tax. It overlooked the marina, had an outdoor pool, spa, restaurant, and several high-end specialty stores. I was ready to leave my room and visit all the hotel amenities the next morning, when my phone rang at nine a.m. Sam was on the other end, telling me to get ready for a busy day in La Paz.

Because of the early start he had to appease my grouchy mood by making the rounds at the shops in Cabo. None were as upscale as the boutiques at the hotel, but that didn't stop me from buying a few hokey knick-knacks obviously intended for dumb tourists such as myself. After popping in and out of tacky stores, we hopped in Sam's jalopy for a ride up to La Paz, the capital of the state of Baja South. Once again, it was a town boasting a palatial resort with various residential options clustered around pools, restaurants and beachfront. Because of its 250-slot marina, it also offered its guests ideal access to the Sea of Cortez.

I assumed this paradise was a playground for college spring break revelers or an endless array of time-sharing pitches for the many resorts lining the beach. At the moment, I was satisfied simply immersing myself in the beauty of the sea and the occasional sight of its inhabitants: marlin, giant humpback whales, and a shimmering curtain of nervous sardines.

We stopped for a bite of lunch at a local beach bar where the bartender and waitress greeted Sam with, "Hola, Senor Levine. Bienvenido."

It didn't take a genius to know he was a regular in this thatch-roofed shack. "We have to try this cantina, Lily," he said when we entered La Paz. "The food is as authentic as anything you'll find in these parts."

After a delicious meal of tacos, rice, beans, and warm tortillas, washed down by a couple of Corona Lites, I had to agree. We ate for two hours, all the while listening to Ivy Queen belt out 'Amor Puro' from a pair of loudspeakers behind the counter. Sated with food and atmosphere, we hit the road of ravenous potholes and headed to my hotel. I planned to nap at the pool before visiting the Lizard Lounge that night. Sam was eager for me to meet Jose.

Chapter 20

Wanting to blend with the natives at the Lizard Lounge, I stopped at the hotel boutique after a refreshing nap and purchased a colorful Mexican woven blouse to wear over a pair of jeans. From what Sam described, I didn't expect to find a crowd of overdressed imbibers bellying up to the bar.

After a quick snack at the hotel lounge, I met Sam in the lobby at eight o'clock. "The Lizard really doesn't pick up until nine or so, but I want to introduce you to a couple friends and Rosa before the joint gets too noisy," he said as we entered a cave-like structure of adobe brick.

A neon sign flickered above the front door with the letters 'g' and 'e' missing.

"They'll probably never replace those letters," Sam said as we approached the front door. "Anyone who has been in Cabo for more than a day doesn't need a sign to find this place. It's widely known throughout town as 'the Lizard'."

I couldn't remember if Sam told me Rosa was one of its

barmaids but she was easy to spot. The sexy young girl toting a tray of Coronas between the crowded tables had to be the infamous Rosa. She was a beautiful creature, and it was easy to see how Sam would be drawn to the luminous brown eyes, long, dark hair and body that could put Shakira's to shame. When her tray emptied, she walked toward us, planted a big smooch on Sam's cheek and turned to me.

I'd been warned she spoke very little English, so when she said, "You Sam's hermana mayor," I retuned her broad smile with one of my own.

Her smile lit up her face and showed sparkling white teeth against smooth olive skin.

"Did you tell her I was the mayor of someplace?" I whispered to Sam.

"Hermana mayor means big sister in Spanish," he whispered back. "She's been practicing for a week, so be nice, keep smiling and shake your head 'yes'."

A picture of the two in bed making love with a Spanish-English dictionary between the sheets popped into my mind. It was like a pornographic film I had clicked on the television by mistake.

Clasping Rosa's hand, I said, " Si, si, Senorita Rosa, I am Sam's hermana mayor."

Five minutes later, we were seated in a red vinyl booth with bottles of beer, tortilla chips and a bowl of very hot salsa. An hour passed, and I began to count up the bottles of beer and bowls of salsa we would consume if Jose didn't make his appearance soon. At nine o'clock, Sam motioned toward the door.

"Jose just came in, and he's headed this way," Sam mumbled.

A tall, clean-cut looking man slid into the booth next to Sam. Somehow I expected him to be a short, swarthy, bearded hombre with beady, evil eyes capable of committing the crime that ruined Sam's life. Certainly, not this hunk of sexy masculinity.

"Amigo, who is this lovely lady with you today?"

"Jose, meet an old friend from the States, Lily Lawrence. She's visiting for a few days and I've been giving her a tour of Cabo."

He reached a calloused hand across the table and said, "Welcome. Sam is showing you a good time?"

"Great. The last two days have been paradise. I'm afraid I'll not want to go home. But I have a business to run so I have to make the most of my time here."

Sam kicked me under the table and raised his eyebrows like Groucho Marx. I neglected to tell him I'd cooked up a story that might give us a chance to look at the hot merchandise.

"What sort of business?" Jose asked.

"It's just a small store where I take in household items to

resell. The more unique the better, so I'm always looking for something a little different than what can be found in the States. I thought during my days down here, I might find an accessory or two to bring back. Unfortunately, every shop is full of the usual items—t-shirts, cups, piñatas, and fridge magnets."

"I might be able to help you out," Jose said after he'd killed off of his tequila in one giant swallow.

"How so?"

"Before coming to Mexico, I picked up some interesting items in California and brought them down here to sell."

"Really? I'd love to see them, and if they are right for my store, maybe we can work out a deal. I can't buy anything too heavy or difficult to carry on the plane, and, of course, price is an issue."

I gave Sam a quick glance. He looked apoplectic. "That's okay with you, isn't it, Sam?"

He gave me another kick under the table. "Sure, why not? Since when have you started asking my advice about your business?"

"Good, then come to my hotel tomorrow, Jose. Bring whatever merchandise you think I can use in the shop and maybe we can make a deal."

"Time to get you back to the hotel, Lily. You've had more than your share of tequila," Sam said.

I shook Jose's hand, gave him the name of my hotel, and said I'd see him at noon the next day.

"Manana, Lily," he replied.

We were barely out the door when Sam gave me his look that could kill.

"What the hell was that all about?"

"You said some of the stuff he's trying to sell might be from your home robbery and I thought this would be a good way to see it. After all, I'm just a little old lady selling used junk who may buy his hot merchandise."

"Sorry for yelling at you, Lily, but your story about having a shop threw me for a loop. Then you ask him to your hotel room to look at his loot? I think living in that Home has affected your good sense. And don't think for one minute that I won't be there when Jose arrives. Besides, you don't know what was taken in the robbery so I have to identify the pieces that will nail this guy."

We agreed Sam should come to my room before Jose's arrival. Pulling up to the hotel, I barely heard him say, "I know you're doing this for me, and aside from your crazy tactics, I want you to know I love you for it, Big Sister."

I kissed him on the cheek. "See you manana, Senor Levine."

Chapter 21

Determined to be on hand when Jose came with his bag of goodies, Sam arrived at the hotel before 11:30, and started dispensing advice on how to conduct myself with Jose. His officious demeanor reminded me of the old days when we'd go on a surveillance job.

"Now remember, Lily, if I don't recognize any of his stuff, I'll have a coughing spell as a signal not to buy anything. If I see a familiar object, I'll make a big fuss about its worthiness so you can start the bargaining process. If you pay for something, make sure you get a receipt with his signature. Once I have proof of his participation in the robbery, I'll try to get information about this Pablo Gutierrez because, according to Jose, he's the one who killed Rebecca."

As usual, Sam was hungry and thirsty so we ordered room service for three. In a creepy way, Jose was our guest, so we decided to feed him, too.

"No beer, Sam. It's way too early to start on booze.

Besides, you have to be mentally sharp this afternoon. So what shall we order, coffee or Mexican cocoa?"

As I expected, he opted for coffee to accompany the huevos rancheros, which arrived minutes before Jose knocked on the door. A big, bulky duffel bag hung over his shoulder and he clutched a smaller briefcase in his hand.

"Buenas tardes," he greeted us, while looking around the room.

If he thought we had the Mexican police waiting, he was instead pleasantly surprised to spot the tray of huevos rancheros.

"Ah, the aroma of my favorite food. Am I invited to partake or must we get down to business?"

"Let's eat first or the eggs will get cold," Sam said. "And we don't want to rush looking through your merchandise."

Jose and Sam sat on the only two chairs in the room while I perched on the side of the bed, balancing my plate of eggs. Eager to get the meal finished, I ate quickly. Jose took his time, wiping up every morsel of food and draining every last drop of coffee.

He finally wiped his mouth and said, "A very nice way to begin the business matter at hand."

Strolling over to the duffle bag tossed by the door, he brought it to the bed and turned its contents onto the multi-colored spread. Holy shit, he had enough merchandise to stock a Wal-Mart.

Sam gazed at the array on the bed and asked, "Where the hell did you get all this?"

I assumed it was meant to be a rhetorical question since Sam knew exactly where the loot was obtained.

"Some from my escapades in the States, and the cheaper goods I got here in Cabo."

More than likely, he picked up a thing or two from the unsuspecting tourists he'd befriended at the Lizard Lounge and other hot spots where thieves plied their trade. A lot of cheap costume jewelry, gaudy necklaces strung with a potpourri of imitation gems, crowded out the expensive Rolex or two, and a diamond ring.

But the most notable item, like an elephant in the room, was a gold menorah smack in the middle of the jewelry collection. Sam picked up the piece and turned it over. He stared at the bottom for what seemed a very long time, then handed it to me. In small italic letters, an inscription read, "To my dear Sam and Rebecca. Many years of happiness."

From the expression on Sam's face, I feared for Jose's life. But his outward appearance belied his words. "Now where would you find a piece of junk like this?"

"Oh, that's not junk, my amigo. A pawnbroker in Oakland told me it is probably worth a couple hundred dollars. I was afraid selling it to him would trip me up with the cops."

"Why would this simple candle holder get you in trouble with the police?" Sam's voice came out confident and sure.

"We got it from a house in Frisco where my pal, Pablo, shot some lady."

Holding the candelabra, with one high and eight additional prongs, Sam looked as if he was seeing it for the first time. I didn't know a lot about Jewish tradition, but I had heard the menorah symbolized that all people are equal, and enhance mankind's connection with God. *How ironic that this spiritual piece would bring down a thief and murderer.*

"I'd like to buy this" Sam said, "How about fifty dollars?"

"Man, it's worth at least twice as much. How about one-hundred?"

Sam was playing hard-to-get, but not wanting to screw up the deal, he agreed to the one-hundred and peeled off the bills. "Okay here are the hundred bucks. Now I need a signed receipt as proof I paid you with cash."

"No problem, Amigo. I have a receipt book with me."

"How about you, Senora? See anything that interests you?"

"Not really. Sam bought the best in your cache."

"Okay, your loss. Maybe I'll see you both tonight at the Lizard Lounge?"

"Sure," we said in unison.

We were feeling smug and satisfied when Jose stuffed his duffle bag with the remaining loot and left.

Chapter 22

The moment Jose left the room I gave Sam a bear hug. "Finally, you have proof of the robbers. Now what?"

"Before getting the Mexican police involved, I need to find Pablo, the shooter. If he hears Jose is locked up, he could disappear from the face of the earth and I may never find him. Since I'm now one of Jose's customers, it may be easier to get more details from him about Pablo's whereabouts. You want to join me at the Lizard Lounge tonight?"

"I wouldn't miss it for the world."

Because I had only two days left in Mexico, I insisted on buying Sam dinner at the Caffe Todos Santos. The restaurant, recommended by the concierge at my hotel, for its pleasant patio, good food, and touristy prices, would be the perfect place to celebrate our successful afternoon. After dinner, we left for the Lizard Lounge where Jose was already established on a stool buying drinks for the house. The roll of bills Sam paid him for the menorah lay on the bar.

"Buenas noches, Senor Sam," Jose slurred. "And senorita," he added with a wobbly bow.

He'd obviously consumed a few tequilas, which might be helpful in gleaning information about Pablo's whereabouts. Motioning to a couple stools beside him, he said, "Sit, amigo. And you, too, senorita."

After ordering two Dos Equis, Sam started an animated conversation with Jose. The din of the crowd made it impossible for me to hear the conversation from where I sat, but I picked up a repetitive question now and then.

"Come on, Jose. Where does Pablo live?"

"Why are you interested in my friend?"

Sam leaned close too Jose and whispered something in his ear.

I was still nursing my beer when Sam nudged my arm and said, "Let's get outta here, Lily."

We didn't say a word until we were in the car. "Well, did you get any useful information about Pablo?'

Sam shifted into high gear and took off at a speed I didn't think the decrepit wreck was capable. "You mean after I identified myself and told him he was going down for murder in a home invasion? You bet I found out something, and tomorrow morning I'm going to the local police station to get the wheels rolling on extraditing these two scumbags back to the States.

"Seems that Pablo has been right under my nose, down here in La Paz, contacting Jose almost daily. Apparently, he's either smarter than Jose or less of a boozer, because he warned Jose not to sell any of the loot. But now that I have the menorah as proof of the robbery, and Jose's word that Pablo killed Rebecca, I have no doubt that offering Jose a deal for a lighter sentence is all it will take for him to testify against Pablo at trial."

Sam's adrenaline was flowing. It flooded the old car as he shifted gears with a vengeance, yelled a string of profanities at horse-driven carriage rides, and banged his hand on the steering wheel when traffic stalled on Cabo's main drag.

"Calm down, Sam. You'll never live to be at their trial if you have a heart attack or stroke. I know you've held your rage back for a long time, but going bonkers now isn't going to get these guys in jail any sooner.

"With your contacts in law enforcement, I know you'll see an end to this soon. I have a flight out of here day after tomorrow; so while you're getting the situation wrapped up, don't worry about entertaining me. I'll amuse myself with last minute sightseeing and shopping. And I can take the hotel shuttle to the airport."

"If that's okay with you, Lily. I probably wouldn't be good company, anyway. At least, let me take you to a farewell lunch tomorrow."

"No, no. Who knows where or what you'll be doing at noon. We'll just say goodbye now and, hopefully, you'll come home as soon as possible. Then, while Jose and Pablo are sitting in jail, we'll have a celebratory dinner at the best restaurant in San Francisco. Maybe, we can celebrate the Journey's End killer's capture, too," I added wistfully.

At the hotel's entrance, I gave him a teary kiss on the cheek. "Good luck, Sam."

"Good luck to you, too, big sister."

I spent my last day in Cabo roaming the quaint shops, buying myself a lovely scarf in memory of Monique, and for Lloyd, who was taking in my newspaper, I bought a tacky white t-shirt inscribed "Cabo San Lucas." Throughout my week's vacation, not a day passed when I didn't think of that white cashmere sweater. And, each time, I found myself struggling with a myriad of 'what ifs.'

Never one to book an early morning flight, I slept until eight the next morning, had a continental breakfast from room service, then rode the shuttle to the airport and my noon departure. With flying time only a little over three hours to the Bay Area, I would be at the Home by late afternoon. I wasn't looking forward to my return.

Being involved in Sam's adventure had been exciting

and fulfilling. The time away from the confines of Journey's End had also given me a sense of release and freedom. But it was time to once again delve into the nefarious events that had taken place behind it walls. I owed it to my friend, Monique.

Chapter 23

My week away from the Home did nothing to abate my discontent with Journey's End. Everything was exactly as when I had left — same food, same parking space, and same noise emanating from the couple upstairs. I knew one of the answers to my unhappiness would be finding the serial killer roaming its hallways and then getting the hell out of Dodge.

First, I had to satisfy my recent nagging doubts about Lloyd. My newly aroused suspicions only added to my depression. For months I'd counted on him as a friend and trusted dinner companion. Now, I couldn't get the picture of his white cashmere sweater out of my mind. Somehow I must get a snippet of it to compare with the thread I found in the bushes.

The opportunity arose the following week when Armanda asked me to change my regular Thursday morning housecleaning with Lloyd's Thursday afternoon. Switching days or times for cleaning apartments was a common occurrence, often due to lack of staffing, or sometimes just on the whim of Marlene, the housekeeping supervisor, who had been with Journey's End forever and practically ran the place. I readily agreed, already plotting a ruse for getting into his apartment while Armanda was inside.

Thursday morning I awoke with much trepidation. About ten o'clock when I knew Armanda would be hard at work in the fourth floor penthouse, I walked up the stairs to the apartment. As the housekeeping crew was inclined to do, the door was left slightly ajar with a rolled up towel. I heard water coming from a hose on the large patio where she was watering plants. Cleaning and watering outdoor spaces was one of the perks for living in an expensive penthouse apartment. So far, I had perfect timing.

Wearing fluffy, soft Dearform slippers, I was able to enter the living room without a sound and headed for the master bedroom. Sure that Lloyd would never hang an expensive sweater on a hanger, I started to look through drawers in the heavy walnut dresser. One held neatly folded boxer shorts. In another, socks were rolled up like tennis balls, segregated by color, and lined up in little rows. After five minutes, I was learning more about Lloyd's OCD by rifling through his dresser drawers, than I had on our Friday night dates.

Although I assumed the matching armoire at the foot of the bed held another mammoth TV, I decided to take a look. Much to my surprise and delight, three shelves held clothes--an assortment of tees, dress shirts in plastic laundry bags, and several sweaters of various colors. Voila! On the bottom shelf I spotted the white cashmere he had worn to my apartment.

So engaged with my sudden find, I didn't hear the hose turn off on the patio, and the water turn on in the kitchen. There was no time to snip off a piece of thread with the manicure scissors in my pocket, so I grabbed the entire sweater. Quietly closing the armoire, I made a run for the front door. Armanda was at the kitchen sink, scrubbing the stainless steel, and humming a few bars of JLo's recent hit.

The stairwell, only a few steps away, took me to my apartment within minutes. I hadn't accomplished what I set out to do—snip a tiny thread from the sweater, and had complicated matters by taking the entire sweater. But, there was nothing I could do about the situation now, except hope that Lloyd was truthful when claiming he seldom wore this particular sweater. If true, it wouldn't be missed for months. Hopefully, by then, I would have it back in the armoire.

From my jewelry box on the dresser, I opened the small baggie in which I placed the strand of wool retrieved from the bushes, and held it against a sleeve of the soft white sweater. There was no doubt it was a perfect match. However, as Sam was likely to say, it wasn't the smoking gun needed to accuse Lloyd of anything other than having expensive taste in outerwear. There were probably similar sweaters in closets throughout Journey's End. Still, the fiber match was enough to give me doubts about Lloyd, and good reason to pursue details of his former life.

I knew his former business career was financial planning, but he never mentioned a company name. Without that, how the hell could I get anywhere in my Google search? Starting with the obvious, I entered his name. The resulting data was information I already knew. His age, seventy-two, his aunts, Alice and Beatrice Bellingham in Iowa, and various places he'd lived—Marin County, Iowa, and San Diego.

Not willing to pay $59.95 for additional information, which included bankruptcies, etc., I decided to wait for Sam's return home. He could contact his old pals at the SFPD who could get the information for free. I hadn't heard from him since returning from Cabo, but assumed he was tying up loose ends with Rosa, Jose, Pablo and the Mexican police. I called his apartment in Oakland and left a message to get back to me ASAP, as I needed him urgently.

A few days later, I picked up a ringing telephone to find Sam on the other end of the line. "The connection is so clear, you sound right next door," I said after expressing my joy at hearing from him.

"Almost, Lily. I returned to Oakland yesterday, after

going through one of the most emotional cases of my career. Sorry I didn't return your call sooner, but I needed some time to get back to normal."

"I understand. Now tell me some good news. Are Jose and Pablo in jail?"

"Not just any jail, but the one in San Francisco where they're awaiting trial. With the evidence, and the threats I made about being charged for murder if he didn't give Pablo up, Jose broke down and told me everything. He said Rebecca walked in while they were trashing the house; Pablo panicked, pulled out a .35 and shot her. That confession was all I needed to get the Mexican police involved. By then, the scum bags wanted an immediate extradition to the States rather than spend any time in a Mexican jail."

"Oh, Sam, I'm so glad you finally have some justice for Rebecca."

"I'll feel totally at peace when they're convicted and serving time in San Quentin. Now tell me what's going on with you at the old people's home. Anymore killings?"

"No. But I may have a new suspect, and you won't believe who it might be."

"Well, let's see. I can start by eliminating anyone over ninety or on a walker or wheelchair. So whom does that leave? About one-tenth of the men there?"

"Quit being an asshole, and let me tell you the piece

of evidence I found from the last person I would have dreamed might be the culprit."

I proceeded to tell Sam about my search through the rhododendron bushes where Mrs. Wilson was killed, and my discovery of a thin, white cashmere thread that matched Lloyd's sweater. I didn't mention I saw him in the sweater at my apartment, nor did I inform him that the suspicious sweater was now in my possession. Knowing Sam, he'd feel compelled to make a nasty remark about senior hanky-panky going on between Lloyd and me.

"Lily, Lily. I know that for years I told you to be suspicious of everybody and everything, but you have, literally, one thread to hang serial murders on someone. What's the motive? Does he have a criminal background? And, besides, you told me he was a nice guy who took you out to dinner and pushed you around in your wheelchair when you had foot surgery, so why would he go around killing other old ladies in wheelchairs?"

I resented his comment about 'other old ladies,' but let it slide because I needed his help. "That's where you come in, Sam. I'm getting nowhere on the Internet because I don't know where to look other than Google. You have resources like VICAP and people at the FBI. Don't some of these guys owe you a favor for something? As a matter of fact, you just solved a cold case of home invasion and murder. Granted, it was personal, but it was you who got it off the books."

There was a long resigned sigh on the other end of the line, and I knew he was hooked. "Okay, Lily. I'll pick up where I left off with my friends at SFPD, and see if they've done anything, although I doubt it. I'll call Bob Kasinsky at the local FBI office, too, and see if he'll take a look at pending cases. But you have to give me more than just this guy's name. Where he was born, lived, worked. Anything you know about his past would help make me sound less like a frustrated PI."

After telling Sam everything Lloyd told me over our wine-sodden dinners, I said, "Please keep me updated on anything you find. If this whole situation is far-fetched, I promise to let it drop, then get the hell out of here and join a nunnery."

"I believe you're desperate enough to move out of that place, but I'm afraid a nunnery would have to be pretty desperate to accept you."

Now, that was a depressing thought.

Chapter 24

In Sam's follow-up call to my request, he said his high-ranking friend at the FBI was busy chasing down a potential terrorist, but he spoke to another agent, Ms. Mallory, who would do what she could to help out.

"She gave me some general information I think may be of interest to you. After telling her your friend was a financial advisor, she told me that financial abuse of the elderly is a serious and common crime perpetrated throughout the United States.

"And most scams against elderly people are done by one individual, usually a family member or other trusted person with access to financial information. These scam artists often call themselves 'certified trust advisors' or estate planning experts, but they are not experts and usually not certified by anyone.

"You did tell me this Lloyd fellow was in the investment business, right?"

"Yes. He said he worked for a company in San Diego and then opened up his own office here in Marin County."

"Well, if his business dealings weren't kosher and some seniors got financially harmed, you might have a motive. But I can't imagine why it would affect people at the Home. Let me do a little more checking with some of the numerous legal protections in California that look out for victims. Unfortunately, safeguards are rarely invoked, and when they are, relief is difficult to come by. But I'll give the Federal Trade Commission and Department of Commerce and Consumer Affairs a call to see what I can find out. Meanwhile, you do a little interrogating of this Lloyd character in a non-threatening way. I know how you can get, Lily, when your antenna is up, so cool it when you talk with him."

My opportunity for further conversation with Lloyd came the following Friday when we had dinner for the first time since my return from Baja. He had selected a lovely restaurant on the water in Tiburon. And I suppose to show his appreciation for my remembering him while on vacation, he wore the tee shirt emblazoned with 'Cabo San Lucas' under a blue blazer. We had our first glass of wine and an appetizer at a window table before moving into the main dining room.

Lloyd pestered me to tell him everything I'd done on my vacation, so I related my week of adventures, excluding any mention of Jose or Pablo. I told him Sam had given me a grand tour of the Baja Peninsula (true), and that we spent a lot of time on the beach or in the water (not true). I failed to mention Sam's stolen menorah, or hours spent at the Lizard Lounge reeling in suspicious expats who were now languishing in the San Francisco jail.

"Enough about me and my trip. How about we spend a little time talking about you?" I said. "You must have had some interesting clients while working as an investment advisor. Maybe a Donald Trump or Warren Buffett type? In affluent places like San Diego and Marin County, you probably ran into some really high rollers."

"Actually, I dealt more with the middle-class senior population, helping them find steady retirement income and ways to shield investments from capital gains taxes. I suppose that's why I decided to retire at Journey's End. I became familiar with the senior population and their place in the community."

"Sounds pretty noble. Maybe I should have consulted someone like you a few years ago so I wouldn't sweat out the big check I write to the Home every month."

"If my license hadn't expired, I'd be happy to give you advice, Lily, but I don't think the Department of Corporations would approve if I tried to sell you any kind of investment now."

"What does the Department of Corporations have to do with financial advice?"

"Everything. Their principle duty is to provide protection to consumers engaged in financial transactions. They also license and regulate securities brokers and dealers, investment advisers and financial planners, such as myself."

"Unfortunately, I never thought much about money or saving for a rainy day. The only reason I'm experiencing a little financial insecurity now is that, looking around the Home, I see these people who seem to have tons of money stashed away. Makes me feel like the poor kid on the block."

"Don't be fooled by outward appearances, Lily."

I contemplated his comment for just a moment. *Truer words were never spoken by someone who should know.*

Our veal piccata arrived and we devoured it without indulging in more conversation. After finishing the bottle of wine and refusing dessert, I still hadn't gotten far in engaging Lloyd to talk for the past two hours. So I used a different approach on the ride home.

"As a Midwesterner, you probably played a lot of football in college. I know you like watching sports, so I imagine you played some in school."

"I wasn't into playing sports, but I do like to watch the games, especially college football."

"Have you done much traveling since retirement? Ever visited Mexico? Italy?'

I was determined to hear something personal about this guy.

"For some reason, I've never been interested in hopping on and off airplanes simply to spend a couple weeks in a foreign country."

The man was sounding more and more like the nerd I pegged him for when he surprised me by saying, "I dabbled a bit in horse racing for a while, and owned a filly in San Diego."

"You owned a race horse? Now, that's exciting. Where did it race?

"Mostly at Del Mar in San Diego, but the nag never did all that well."

Slowly and painfully, I discovered a few more details about the mysterious Lloyd. He played golf for a while until developing bursitis in his shoulder. "Actually, I hated the game, and only played because of business contacts."

I finally gave up. Aside, from his race horsing days, his past was as boring as his present. And I certainly hadn't gleaned anything incriminating to pass on to Sam.

Just before reaching Journey's End, he broke our silence by asking, "You've had Armanda as a housecleaner, right?"

"Yes, since I moved in. She's great."

"Did you ever suspect her of stealing anything?"

"Armanda? Absolutely not. Why do you ask?"

"Because I'm missing a very expensive sweater, and I could swear it was in my armoire just a few weeks ago."

Thinking fast, I said, "Maybe you sent it to the cleaners and forgot to pick it up."

"I don't wear it much, so I'm sure it didn't need cleaning."

"Maybe you put it someplace other than the armoire."

"Maybe."

Holy shit! As long as I'd known the man, he wore that sweater only twice— to my apartment one night and maybe the morning he killed Mrs. Wilson in the rhododendron bushes. So why was he suddenly concerned as to its whereabouts?

The next day, I called Sam with the measly bit of information I gathered the night before. "Maybe the fact that he dealt primarily with seniors as a financial advisor, and his connection with the Del Mar Race Track in San Diego will help your friend at the FBI," I said hopefully.

"You did good, Lily. I'll pass on the info to Ms. Mallory first thing Monday, but don't get your hopes up. A case like this takes time, especially when it's not top priority."

Maybe not top priority to the FBI, but it certainly was with me.

Meanwhile, since Lloyd and I still had the semblance of some sort of relationship, I continued to dig deeper into his past. I knew the home he sold before moving to Journey's End was in one of the more expensive neighborhoods of Marin County, and before the housing melt down, he probably sold it for several million dollars. His penthouse at the Home was priced over a million, and he recently bought a brand new Lexus.

No doubt an interior decorator charged him a pretty penny to design the three bedroom, two bath apartment, and he always had play-money for the pricey restaurants we frequented.

All this expensive living indicated a successful career, which led me to conclude that he advised only wealthy clientele on how to invest their money. If I could find a former client or two, I'd have an understanding of how he ran his business, which seemed to be his only life before Journey's End.

On my volunteer day at the American Cancer Society, I heard the county was in need of volunteers. Maybe I would have access to information on criminal activities if I worked in the DA's office at the Civic Center. I had plenty of free time and another four-hour volunteer job wouldn't interfere with my non-existent social life.

A week later, I sat across the desk from the county's Volunteer Coordinator. "You've had significant experience with a private investigator, I see," she said after looking over my resume, "so I can certainly place you with the District Attorney's Office, as you requested. They're always in need of what we call a "floating" volunteer, someone who goes to different offices swamped with cases. How does that sound to you?"

It sounded perfect. I would be smack in the middle of all the criminal action that happened or was about to happen in the county. Who knew what I would learn?

"I love variety. When would you like me to start?"

The following Wednesday afternoon, I found myself in a small cubicle, with Assistant D. A. Joan Barbero, typing up a brief for an upcoming misdemeanor trial involving petty theft and disorderly conduct. Sam and I handled cases like this on a daily basis, so Joan (she insisted we use first names) was very impressed with my legal know-how.

"You seem quite familiar with the law, Lily," she told me after I worked with her for a couple of weeks. "Ever work for a lawyer?"

"Never for a lawyer but I was an assistant to a private investigator for a very long time. As a former cop in San Francisco, he knew the law pretty well and could have been a lawyer himself. He also loved sharing his knowledge, and taught me a lot about the business of crime."

Except how to find a serial killer in the very building in which I lived.

Chapter 25

Within a short time, my new volunteer job became the highlight of my week. Not only because it took me away from the Home for a few hours on Wednesdays, but I was once again in the world I loved when working with Sam.

I never knew from assignment to assignment which ADA I'd be assisting, as the caseloads changed almost overnight. In my 'training' period, I stayed with Joan while she cleared a backload of misdemeanor cases—reckless driving, petty thefts, drug possession, and vandalism. Each case was interesting, but I was eager to work with an ADA who handled felonies, preferably murder cases. Fortunately, for the community, murder did not occur often in tony Marin County.

A month after I'd been assigned to Joe Pastori, a top prosecutor in the District Attorney's office, one of his new cases caught my attention. A sixty-two year old man from a nearby area was facing an upcoming trial for running a Ponzi scheme. The embezzler captured a lot of media attention because of his two thousand victims statewide—considered one of the largest Ponzi schemes in state history. The defendant was arrested after a seventeen-month investigation. Pastori was prepping for a lengthy trial with the possibility of the defendant serving more than fifty years in prison.

But on the eve of his long-delayed trial, the son-of-a-bitch reached a plea bargain with the DA's office, in exchange for a ten-year prison sentence. The public was outraged, particularly the victims in the case. One Marin County elderly investor told the local paper, "I don't think ten years is enough for what he's done to people's lives. He should have to do at least twenty years."

Another elderly victim said, "That swindler is getting off easy compared to sentences of more than a hundred years given to others like Bernie Madoff and Allen Sanford."

Considering the woman had lost at least half of the $600,000 she invested, everyone who knew anything about the case agreed. I, too, was outraged at the penalty handed down and let my boss know it.

"How in the world could this have happened to so many people?" I asked him one day shortly after the trial was over.

"During the run up of the real estate market, there were plenty of new investors looking for steady retirement income and ways to shield investments from capital gains taxes," Pastori said. "The victims, many of them seniors, said they were assured their money was safe and would earn them steady monthly returns of eight to twelve percent. But after the housing bubble burst, new investors dried up and previous investors stopped receiving monthly payments."

Why did his words ring a bell? Weren't those the exact words Lloyd used when I asked about his investment business? I could still hear his answer: *"I dealt with the middle-class senior population, helping them find steady retirement income and ways to shield investments from capital gains taxes."*

I didn't know if Lloyd Bellingham's financial business was based on a "rob Peter to pay Paul" scam, but I finally had some insight into how a financial motive might lead to murder. Senior after senior citizen reported stories of financial hardship as the result of being suckered into false promises. Unfortunately, many more were reluctant to tell their stories because of shame at their own gullibility.

"It hurts big time when you've lost as much as I have," one woman said after discovering she lost her entire retirement savings.

But that scumbag hadn't killed any victims of his dishonest schemes. So why would someone attempting the same type of offense feel compelled to commit the ultimate crime of taking a life, particularly against helpless old women? Sam once told me that killing was about power, loss of self-control, or removing a problem. Which of these could be motive for the Journey's End killer?

After the Ponzi scheme case, I was sent to the misdemeanor offices again because Joan had grown fond of me, and claimed she needed help dealing with a passel of minor crimes. Arguably the most varied misdemeanor is indecent exposure, because the term "indecent" can mean many different things. Legally, it was defined as intentionally exposing his or her person to another with the knowledge that the action could cause reasonable alarm. I thought the indecent exposure crime might be interesting, but before Joan received any of the sordid details, it was handed off to Joe Pastori. Turned out the stupid bloke exposed his pecker to a minor, qualifying him as a felon.

During days I was free of commitments, and in the evenings after my volunteer stints, I continued my search on the Internet for some remote clue connecting the three victims. I'd not been a friend to Mrs. Wilson or Mrs. Shaw, so I had little knowledge of either lady. And because Monique spent most of her life abroad, there were few details, aside from her life on the stage, which gave me insight into her activities while she lived in the States. When her cousin came to make arrangements for burial, he did tell me there was a French husband for a short while, one who she conveniently forgot to mention. The marriage ended many years ago, so, like my ex-husbands, he was probably out of sight and out of mind.

But finding the ex-husband gave me an idea. Who would know more about someone's personal, financial, and emotional dealings than a relative? Children, siblings, ex-husbands, even long-time friends might have an answer as to what connected Mrs. Wilson, Mrs. Shaw and Monique in a way that would lead to murder.

I had a telephone number for Monique's cousin in France, but before telephoning Jacques, I should be prepared with succinct and useful questions. No sense wasting money on an international call if it didn't provide useful information. And, I definitely didn't want him knowing my suspicions about Monique's manner of death.

For insight on the other two women, I needed to talk with their closest friends at the Home. So one day, I sauntered down to lunch and spotted them in the dining room.

Approaching their table, I said, "Excuse me for disturbing your lunch, but I have a small favor to ask. Out of forgetfulness, I never sent sympathy cards to relatives when Mrs. Wilson and Mrs. Shaw died, so I'd like to send a condolence note to the family. As my mother used to say, "Better late than never."

Their response to my request was less congenial than expected. "You'll just dredge up terrible memories if you send a condolence card now," Mrs. Shaw's best friend,

Caroline, murmured, looking as if I said an exhumation was necessary.

After assuring her I would be tactful and courteous when contacting the family, she reluctantly agreed to put phone numbers and addresses of Mrs. Shaw's relatives in my mail box the next day.

Mrs. Wilson's friend, Alice, was more horrified and vocal at my request. "What a nerve you have, wanting to contact grieving people all these months after Shirley's death," she hissed through her thin, tight mouth. "Do you have any common decency? One does not express sympathy almost a year after the death of a loved one. Besides, I saw you speaking with her daughter at the memorial."

In retrospect, my excuse for wanting to contact relatives at this point in time did appear feeble and insensitive, but what was I to say? "I'm looking for a killer of these women and thought a relative might know of someone who would want to harm them?"

For now, they would have to live with the assumption, determined from the day I moved into Journey's End, that Lily Lawrence was a self-centered, uncaring bitch.

Chapter 26

Before I had the opportunity to contact any relatives of the murdered ladies, another strange event occurred at Journey's End.

Dr. Irv Rosenberg, a retired, well-known heart surgeon, was found dead in the Home's gym. I really liked and admired the man, as we had worked out together many times—me on the treadmill and Irv on the recumbent machine. He'd whiz into the gym every morning on his motor scooter, slide from it onto the equipment, and peddle for thirty minutes. On the days we shared the gymnasium, he couldn't abide a blaring television, preferring to carry on a lively conversation ranging from politics, news of the day, the health care system, even gossip at the Home. Although pushing ninety, and frail in body, he loved to let everyone know he still had the mind of a genius.

One night, after months passed in normalcy at Journey's End, a security guard, strolling around the building about nine o'clock, saw a light burning in the gym. After entering the room, he discovered Dr. Irv slumped between his motorized scooter and the recumbent, his head resting on the machine's front panel from which blood pooled on the floor.

After alerting the Sheriff's office, Dr. Irv was transported to the morgue, where the coroner did an autopsy the following day. His finding was "death from blunt force trauma." He also established time of death about seven that evening.

Once again, I knew that was bullshit. Even Dicky questioned why a smart man like Irv would deviate from his routine, and venture to the gym after dinner when most of the residents were going to bed.

"I know why you're here, Lily," Davis said when I entered his office the following day, "And, for a change, I agree with you. Nothing makes sense about Dr. Rosenberg's accident. He was a smart, careful man who would never go to the gym at that time of night."

What a relief! When I expressed doubts over the other accidents to Dicky, he'd treated me as if I was losing my mind, so I never mentioned my suspicions to him again. It took the strange death of the Home's most respected resident to open his mind that something was rotten inside Journey's End.

"I'm not saying I believe the other deaths were anything

but accidents. The coroner gave a correct ruling on those, but with Dr. Rosenberg, I'm not so sure."

Because he'd conceded something bad might have happened at the "finest retirement living in the Bay Area," I held myself back from arguing with him. More importantly, I had another mysterious death for Deputy Thompson, Sam, and other skeptics to ponder.

I immediately called Sam to tell him of Journey's End latest "accident," and to check on what he was doing to help solve these killings.

"I've got Ms. Mallory at the FBI doing background checks on that Wallace guy, and I'll be giving her everything you told me about your friend, Lloyd Bellingham."

The previous memorials for other departed souls at the Home could not compare with the send-off for Dr. Irving Rosenberg. It was held in the auditorium of the San Francisco teaching hospital where he accomplished some of his most impressive work, with only his closest contemporaries invited.

A day after the memorial, I called the sheriff's office and asked to speak with Deputy Thompson. A pleasant young lady told me he was out and wouldn't return until the next day.

"Just tell him Lily Lawrence called about another

strange death at the Journey's End Retirement Home. He should also know that Richard Davis, the CEO here, is very suspicious of what transpired."

Maybe that bit of news would entice him to return my call.

I left my telephone number and said, "I'll be volunteering for the District Attorney tomorrow, so I could drop in to see him. It won't be a problem because his office is practically next door to Deputy Thompson."

"I don't think a drop-in is possible. But I will relay this message to him, and one of us will get back to you."

Was she patronizing me? Would she even give Thompson the message? And what if he didn't return my call? Should I continue to pursue his help or forget about the sheriff's office and talk to Joe Pastori? I felt my fear of rejection kick in and pushed it from my mind.

Was it any wonder I was becoming paranoid? I felt like a hamster on a wheel, spinning, spinning, spinning and getting nowhere fast. At the moment, Sam's connections at the FBI held the most hope for solving these killings. Hopefully, someday in my lifetime.

Chapter 27

Within the next week, everything changed. The first positive result was a return call from Deputy Thompson. He wanted to discuss the recent "accident" of Dr. Rosenberg, as he considered the accident of a man curious, inasmuch as the other deaths had all been women.

"That's a significant change in a killer's MO, if, in fact, there is a killer," he said. Obviously, spurred on by hearing that Mr. Davis suspected foul play in Dr. Rosenberg's death, he put more credence in my suspicions.

"I'd like to talk with your CEO about any resident he thinks capable of murder. What is his name again?"

I had my doubts that Dicky would admit he didn't know the residents well, with the exception of whiners like Lily Lawrence. And he certainly would never admit to the sloppy vetting of new residents.

"Why don't you give me his telephone number and I'll call him today?"

Adding to my good feelings that I was finally getting somewhere with local officials was the unexpected news I received later in the day from Sam.

He reported in with a tip from his friend at the FBI, Ms. Mallory.

"She can't find a Lloyd Bellingham in any of their data files, but she did some snooping on investment businesses in California, and found an LGB Investments, Inc. in San Diego and Marin County Didn't you tell me those were two places your friend worked?"

"Well, yes. But a lot of investment advisors worked in those areas."

"The name doesn't match, anyhow, because the business was owned by a man called Lawrence Brennan. He's a shady character who was fired in 1993 from one of the big insurance companies for forging client's signatures, falsifying ledger statements, and writing checks to himself. He was also fined $50,000 and banned as an investment advisor by the Department of Corrections. It's usually impossible to track these illicit doings unless complaints are filed by clients."

"Why isn't the government on top of these crooks?"

"Impossible, when there are approximately 20,000 licensed investment advisors and 120,000 on the Internet. But Mallory said she'll keep digging and get back to me."

I was beginning to have stronger and stronger misgivings

about my good friend, Lloyd. So many things pointed in his direction. On the other hand, this was the man who rescued me from total isolation when I was wheelchair-bound. This was also the man who helped at the local hospital and worked many hours at his church. And, without this thoughtful man, I would be eating tilapia on Friday nights at the Home. No. Ms. Malloy's findings must be a coincidence. Besides, she said the scammer's name was Lawrence Brennan.

At dinner the next Friday, I'd slip the odd coincidence into my ramblings. I could casually say my friend Sam heard of an investment firm called LGB in San Diego from a past client who was looking for the owner. The subject might open up a discussion, which would either dissolve my qualms or deepen them.

But I never had a chance to pursue that possibility, because for the first time since we started Friday nights on the town, Lloyd called Thursday to cancel our dinner date.

"I have to fly to Iowa and help my Aunt Alice," he said. "She had hip surgery and has no one to care for her when she returns home."

Disabled aunt? Couldn't he come up with a more original excuse than the one used by every man in the world who planned some dilly-dallying? With the fleeting thought he was dumping me for someone younger and cuter with a size D bra cup, my doubts about him disappeared. As a woman, keeping my man faithful to our sexless weekly dates became my primary concern.

"That's too bad about your aunt." I tried to sound sympathetic.

"I'm sure she'll be okay, but with no other relative except her aging sister, she'll need my help for a few days."

Having been a recipient of Lloyd's caring nature, maybe he was one of the few men who actually had a sick aunt. It would be like him to travel thousands of miles to assist an ailing relative.

"How long will you be gone?"

"It depends on how well her recovery goes. She's a tough lady so I suspect she will be up and about quickly. If not, I may find a caretaker to come in."

Actually, his trip was probably the best thing that could happen, except for poor Aunt Alice. With authorities now willing to look into the killings, and a few nebulous clues beginning to pop up, it was better Lloyd not be around.

"I'm leaving on an early morning flight and forgot to notify housekeeping to care for my plants. If the weather becomes warm, would you mind coming up to water the deck plants while I'm gone? I'll drop my apartment key in your mail box before I leave in the morning, if that's okay."

Holy shit! The stars must be in alignment for Librans this week. What a perfect opportunity to not only return the cashmere sweater, but to snoop around a bit.

"Of course I'll water your plants. No problem. I have to warn you, though. I've been accused of being the world's best plant killer."

"I don't think you can do much damage in a week. If I'm still away after a week, Armanda can take over the watering."

"Have a safe trip, tell your Aunt Alice she's in good hands and I wish her well."

Chapter 28

I missed Lloyd. Although we socialized only once a week, he was an escape from the monotony and depression of living at the Home. But my volunteer job was also a wonderful distraction from Journey's End. The few hours spent at the DA's office were filled with interesting people doing meaningful work. Especially intriguing were my assignments with Joe Pastori.

He treated me as if I was more valuable than your typical part-time volunteer, often seeking my opinion on a felony case. The Wednesday after Lloyd left to visit Aunt Alice, Joe asked if I'd like to join him for lunch. One of the volunteer perks was an occasional lunch with the boss in the county cafeteria.

The one place for dining in this vast building was bustling at noon, filled with county workers of all kinds—lawyers, judges, librarians, heads of various departments, as well as deputy sheriffs. With trays in hand, we searched the room for a table when I heard Joe say, "Look, Deputy Thompson is waving us over."

Talk about karmic events! I didn't know whether to be pissed or pleased. If the conversation turned to my talks with Thompson about the strange deaths at Journey's End, how would Joe react? Thus far, he assumed I was intelligent, capable and sharp of mind for an older lady. Would he think differently if Thompson told him my suspicions about Mrs. Wilson, Mrs. Show, Monique and Dr. Rosenberg?

Whatever the outcome, it was too late to worry as we walked to the table where two uniformed deputies sat—Thompson and a red-haired, fair-skinned, baby-faced man who looked more appropriate for a Boy Scout uniform than the blue garb of a deputy sheriff.

Thompson stood up. "Good to see you again, Ms. Lawrence." He shook my hand and introduced the other man. "I'd like you to meet one of our latest hires, Deputy Brady."

"So you know my volunteer?" Joe asked.

"She and I have talked a couple times."

Everyone was busily moving chairs and place settings at the table, which stopped conversation for the moment. I was curious about the deputy's chat with Dicky, but knew this wasn't the time or place to ask. One of these days, I would find out what transpired in that phone call.

Lunch conversation consisted of comfortable discussions about the new deputy, Joe's latest case, and upcoming cutbacks facing each department.

"I'm sure glad I got Brady here before a freeze on hiring goes into effect," Thompson said to Joe. "If things keep up the way they're going, I may have to get a volunteer myself."

"Well, you couldn't do any better than a Lily Lawrence around the office."

Again, I waited for Thompson to tell Joe how pesky I'd been, but he finished his last bite of cherry pie, motioned to Brady, and with another shake of my hand, they took off. Joe didn't ask how I knew Thompson, and I had no intention of telling him.

On our return to the office, Joe said, "Thompson is a helluva nice guy and a great deputy. He tracks down leads like a hound dog."

Strange I hadn't heard any barking dogs since I provided him with four murder leads.

Chapter 29

A couple of days passed since Lloyd left for Iowa and the weather was turning warm—time to perform my watering duties upstairs. I selected a Sunday when the Home became more tomblike than usual. With brunch the only meal served, there was no reason for residents to leave their apartments after one o'clock. As a result, few people wandered the hallways.

I took the back stairs up to Lloyd's unit, unlocked his door with the key he'd left me, and entered the unit. As always, everything was in perfect order. He hadn't left a thing out of place; so after doing my spying, I knew I must leave everything exactly as I found it. Before leaving my apartment, I clipped a thin thread from the sweater I lifted from his apartment, and placed it in the baggie with the strand found in the bushes.

First order of business was returning the carefully folded sweater to the armoire where I found it, and start a search of his office. In the crime TV shows I watched, detectives always started looking through the desk or computer. Either Lloyd didn't own a computer or he took a laptop with him, because there was no sign of any electronic device. It probably didn't matter, because I wasn't a nerdy tech, anyhow. Most likely, I wouldn't get further than "enter password." So I moved on to a big walnut desk dominating the room that was begging to be snooped.

Because I still had to get on the patio where dozens of planted pots waited to be watered, I decided to not waste time in the kitchen, bath or bedroom. Well, maybe I'd give the bathroom medicine cabinet a quick look.

The desk had three drawers on either side and one in the middle, where I started my search. Nothing there but the usual collection of pens, pencils, Post-Its, stapler, scissors, and a datebook. I picked up the black leather planner, and flipped through its pages. Although most days were blank, for the past six months, every Friday night had a scribbled notation, "Dinner with LL."

I found his notation rather endearing, before reminding myself of the duty at hand. Every six months, "dentist cleaning" appeared at two p.m. on Mondays, and there was one reminder of "doctor appointment" in early spring. I flipped through blank pages of the slender book until I reached the day of Mrs. Wilson's death. There, in red ink, I saw the jotting: number '1' followed by the letter 'W' with an exclamation mark. I flipped to the page of the summer picnic. Almost illegible, a scratching appeared in red ink: "Journey's End picnic, '2,' and the letter 'S.'

I quickly found the date of Monique's death. And there it was—a number '3,' the letters 'MM,' and the word, 'scarf.' Goose bumps rose on my arms, and my breath caught in my throat. I moved to the latest entry. A number '4', followed by the word 'Doc', and 'after dinner' appeared in large letters in red ink. There were no exclamation marks.

The bastard had kept a diary of his horrible acts! It was vile and revolting, but it was the clue I'd been hoping to find. No volunteer hours at the church or hospital were noted, making me doubt if they actually existed. His scribbled notations were a revolting, sick reminder of each day he'd taken a life, written by a psychotic killer.

I attempted to open a deep file drawer, but after several unsuccessful attempts, accepted the obvious. The drawer was locked and, unless I found a key, there was no way I could open it without leaving a scratch. The remaining drawers held folders for insurance policies, paid utility invoices, the Journey's End monthly bill, a Medicare supplement, and the usual assortment of papers one accumulates.

Except for the incriminating datebook and locked file drawer, I found nothing else suspicious. The locked drawer intrigued me. It might hold a motive for the killings. But without the means to pry it open, I had to be satisfied with the incriminating day planner.

With datebook in hand, I raced to my apartment. On my HP printer I made copies of the pages with their coded symbols, and then, returned to Lloyd's apartment. I placed the book exactly where I found it, and headed to the patio. After drowning the dozen plants strategically placed in sunny and shady spots, I returned to my apartment feeling only slightly elated. Sure, I found the markings in the date book very significant, but I imagined Sam saying, "What sort of evidence do you call a few scribbles?"

I hoped the notebook was concrete evidence of Lloyd's guilt, but my heart wrestled with glee and disappointment.

Chapter 30

I had to make one more watering trip before Lloyd returned home if his patio plants were to survive. On that final visit, I planned to expand my search of his apartment. Meanwhile, I kept busy with volunteer work—five hours a week in the DA's office and two hours with the American Cancer Society. I still combed through various Internet sites in my spare time, looking for something that would implicate Lloyd as the Journey's End killer.

Now that he had ascended to the top of my suspect list, I stopped looking for the names and pertinent information of other eligible contenders. Bob Wallace was off the hook, as was John, the lonely widower who was already engaged to a resident at the Home. Elton had died from Parkinson's disease the previous month, and Kenny was so weak he was barely able to pick up a fork.

Sitting at the computer on a quiet Saturday afternoon, I came upon a new website entitled, "PUBLIC RECORD SEARCH SERVICE," followed by the words, "Police records, mug shots, contact information and more." How did I miss this gold mine all these months?

I immediately entered Lloyd's name and found nothing. Out of curiosity, I entered the name Lawrence Brennan—the one Sam gave me as owner of LBG Financial Advisors. In order to get access to the full report on Brennan, I broke down and charged my Visa card $59.95, the amount needed to get past the first page. The expense proved worth its cost, for I was soon looking at police reports from San Diego and the Marin Police Department.

The report read like a script from a segment of *America's Most Wanted*. The name Lawrence Brennan showed a long list of improprieties, including his departure from Argonaut Insurance for forgery and falsifying statements and an arrest in 1990. According to the reports, he was facing a lengthy trial and the possibility of more than fifty years in prison when he pleaded no contest to financial fraud, theft and elder abuse in San Diego County in exchange for a ten-year prison sentence. His victims were appalled at the light sentence. As in the case Joe recently prosecuted in Marin, there was fury from the victims for the plea bargain.

The site also included information about the FBI's attempt to find this Brennan character for other crimes against the elderly after his release from jail in 2000. The man's arrogance led him to run another sophisticated scheme in which his victims were left financially and emotionally ruined. Sending out fake statements reflecting healthy stock dividends, selling bogus insurance policies to collect commissions, and boasting of huge company profits when he was the only one profiting, were only a few felonies uncovered thus far.

Brennan was described as a soft-spoken, pleasant man who fabricated accounts, using phony bank and brokerage statements to make it appear he was investing their money, when he was actually underwriting his own expensive lifestyle. According to the latest FBI information, he boasted an upscale home in Marin, maintained a stable of prize thoroughbreds at Del Mar (not one racing filly), and several expensive cars.

Eventually some victims with substantial losses turned to lawyers to file lawsuits, none of which came to fruition because Larry, as his clients knew him, was nowhere to be found. After bilking his elderly clients, few of them had the resources to sustain their legal efforts. The pain and humiliation caused by this man often resulted in sickness, divorce, and even suicide.

The report continued with a caveat from law enforcement officials and victim advocates that white-collar criminals almost always got off with light sentences, if they were ever prosecuted at all. But because the trail of financial ruin left behind by Brennan was so egregious and harmful to the most vulnerable of people, he was at the top of the FBI's financial fugitives list. If any of this related to the man I knew, he was about to face murder charges, too.

I read page after page of the man's wrong doings, and at the end of the list, a high-lighted FBI announcement with an attached photo appeared: IF YOU KNOW THIS MAN OR HIS WHEREABOUTS, PLEASE CONTACT YOUR LOCAL POLICE OR FBI OFFICE.

Was it my imagination or was the grainy, blurry photo a younger Lloyd Bellingham? Admittedly, my mind was working overtime, but take away some of the hair, add a few wrinkles, and the picture bore a close resemblance to the man I considered my good friend. The photo was probably taken at his booking in 1990 when he was jailed for fraud. And because booking photos don't usually show a smile, I was deprived of seeing a mouthful of Chiclet teeth, which would cinch my suspicions.

While congratulating myself on splurging $59.95 for the report, I had to ask "What now?"

Before approaching Deputy Thompson with accusations against Lloyd for not only fraud but also serial killings, I had to call Sam. If Lloyd did commit scams against the four dead residents at Journey's End, it was the perfect motive for murder. After discovering some of the people he'd brought to near financial ruin were his neighbors, and fearing they might alert authorities to his whereabouts, he most likely became desperate when facing the prospect of future jail time.

Chapter 31

I tried calling Sam twice, only to hear, "Sorry I missed your call but leave your name and number and I'll get back to you."

"Sam, call me a soon as you get home. I have something very important to tell you."

When he didn't call back within the hour, I left a more urgent message. "Call me ASAP, Sam. I found something you'll want to hear."

Knowing I was prone to hysterical ravings, he probably would take his sweet time getting back to me, but I sat by the telephone for the rest of the day. At seven that night, my phone rang. Caller ID identified the caller as Sam Levine, and I picked up on the first ring.

"Where the hell have you been? I've been sitting here all day waiting for your call."

"Calm down, Lily. Nothing could be that urgent."

"Oh no? Well, how about if I told you I found out Lloyd Bellingham isn't really Lloyd Bellingham; he's Lawrence

Brennan, former owner of LGB Financial Advisors, one of the FBI's ten most wanted financial criminals."

"Are you making up stories again?"

"No, goddamn it. I went on a website, paid $59.95, and found a ton of information on Bellingham, excuse me, Brennan's criminal past. But the most value for my $59.95 was the mug shot of Brennan. That's how I know it's Lloyd. The booking photo was taken over twenty years ago when he was jailed for fraud, had more hair and less wrinkles, but I know it's him. Take a look for yourself, and tell me what you think. The website is Public Record Search Service, and, if you invest $59.95, you'll find all the stuff I mentioned, including the incriminating photo."

"How will I know if the mug shot is your guy? I've never seen him."

Because Lloyd didn't look like Brat Pitt or George Clooney, I kept him under wraps from my friends on the outside. Shallow must be my middle name, because my first two marriages were based solely on good looks. Sadly, both men lacked character or longevity. Luckily, my third husband possessed both looks and integrity, leading me to believe that one plus in the aging process was an infusion of good sense.

"Oh, I forgot you two haven't met. After you take a look at the mug shot, print it as best you can because it's kind of grainy, and bring it tomorrow night. We'll have dinner in the Home's dining room, and I'll invite Lloyd to join us. He's been curious about you for months so I know he'll say yes."

"Do I have to come for dinner? After hearing your complaints about the food, I'd prefer you make other arrangements for me to meet Lloyd."

"No. This is the best way to make sure I'm right. If you see and talk with him, you'll have a better chance of knowing if the mug shot is Lloyd. Besides, tomorrow night is lamb curry, which is the chef's specialty and one of the better meals.

"I'll bring a nice bottle of wine, so if you don't like the food you can drink your way through dinner. Come to my place at 5:30, and we'll go down to dinner at six."

The bottle of wine must have convinced Sam to come for dinner, because his next complaint was, "Isn't six o'clock a little early to eat?"

"Early? Actually, dinner starts serving at 5:00 here and finishes at seven. But an hour will be all you'll need to determine if I'm right."

"If this is another of your wild goose chases, Lily, I may disown you as a Big Sister."

"Aren't you the one who taught me to trust my instincts? Well, that's exactly what I'm doing, as much as I hate to admit it. I trusted this man, thought he was the nicest, kindest person in the Home, and my only friend after

Monique was gone. So would I really want to believe he was a serial killer?"

Even after I found the strand of thread from the bushes that matched his cashmere sweater, I fought my instincts and chalked it up to a coincidence. Now, with all this other information, the thread and sweater took on a new significance.

"If you're here at 5:30, we'll have time for a drink and I'll fill you in on anything I've forgotten to tell you."

"That, my dear Lily, is a conversation to which I look forward. See you at 5:30."

After hanging up with Sam, I immediately dialed Lloyd's number. "Hi, it's me. My former boss, you know the PI, is coming here tomorrow night for dinner, and I thought you might like to join us."

"Great. I look forward to meeting this man you keep telling me is a top-notch investigator. Besides, it's lamb curry night, one of my favorites. What time should I come to your apartment?"

"Oh no. Just meet us in the lobby at six. I told Sam to be here at five thirty but he has a bad habit of being late for everything."

Tossing and turning that night in bed, I wondered what the hell I was getting everyone into.

Chapter 32

Sam arrived for dinner at exactly 5:30 the following night. When I expressed surprise at his unusual promptness, he admitted it was due to curiosity over my intriguing phone call.

After serving his scotch and soda and my vodka over rocks, I immediately filled him in on my latest discoveries. The baggie with two strands of white cashmere lay on the coffee table, and I had my computer open to the Public Record Search Service page, in the event Sam hadn't bothered to look.

"Did you go on this site?"

"I told you I would."

"Did you print up the mug shot?"

"Yeah, but it's really poor quality. I don't know if I'd recognize anyone from this piece of shit."

"Once you see Lloyd in person, you will notice the resemblance."

I brought Sam up-to-date on my forays into Lloyd's

apartment, and my searches through his desk and closets. "Aside from getting a thread from his sweater, I found some sort of code in his datebook and a locked desk drawer."

"If this guy proves to be your so-called serial killer, he's got quite a record. It's no wonder the FBI have been after him. He's broken every law in the book of the California Business Code, Elder Adult Civil Protection Act, and Consumer Protection Law, just to name a few. And if he is this Lawrence Brennan, and not your knight in shining armor, he's also a killer. Probably the four dead bodies were former clients, and they were a threat to him."

Listening to Sam articulate everything I'd recently determined made me realize what a fool I'd been, and all the months I wasted researching every man at Journey's End, except Lloyd Bellingham. On some selfish level, I couldn't bear the thought of our Friday night dinners coming to an end.

Sam congratulated me on my resourcefulness in combing through the bushes where Mrs. Wilson was found dead. "I see your inquisitive mind is still working."

What is that supposed to mean? Is living in an old people's home supposed to turn me into a retard?

He redeemed himself by saying, "Seems as if I once told you to leave no stone unturned, and with your quirky mind, you expanded it to leave no bush unturned. Good work, Lily. If this guy ever goes to trial, I think every small bit of wool and an incriminating datebook might help the DA's case. As of now, there's no other circumstantial evidence, like prints or DNA."

We finished our drinks, and at six o'clock took the elevator to the lobby. Lloyd was sitting on one of the floral couches, looking uncomfortable and out-of-place. Groups of women were gathered on the sofas and chairs waiting for tardy companions, and when Sam and I approached, all eyes turned to the three of us.

"This is my friend and former boss whom I've spoken so much about," I said to Lloyd as I took Sam's hand and shoved it toward him.

"Nice to meet you, Sam."

"And you're the guy who wined and dined my friend. I understand you kept her from going stir crazy in this place."

I wanted to wring his neck for making such a stupid comment but, instead, said,

"We'd better get to the dining room while there's lamb curry still on the menu."

We sat at a table for three in a far corner of the dining room, and after ordering three lamb curries, Charlie, the headwaiter, opened my bottle of Sauvignon Blanc. Whether it was the wine or something in the curry, Lloyd was more talkative and charming with Sam than he'd ever been with me.

"I imagine being a private investigator is fascinating business," Lloyd said.

"Yeah, you never know from day-to-day what sort of scumbag you'll be hired to tail or investigate."

"Probably a lot of cheating spouses."

"No. I don't like that sort of work. Having been with the SFPD for a number of years, I was often referred to fraud cases, financial crimes, and sometimes a homicide.

"And what did you do before becoming a retired resident of Journey's End?"

I wondered if Sam was setting Lloyd up.

"Nothing as exciting as a PI. I called myself a financial advisor, but always thought of myself as more like a family friend. People trusted me with their future. You know, the kids' college education, home buying, retirement years. I looked upon my job as a great responsibility and an honor—helping people, particularly the elderly, by giving them solid financial advice, suggesting certain investments, annuities, insurance. There's nothing worse than running out of money in your sunset years."

I never heard him wax so eloquently about anything, particularly his former career. It was obvious he was trying to impress Sam.

"To make any real money, you probably had a stable full of wealthy clients."

"No, just ordinary folks, like the sort you see sitting around here."

"Were your offices in Marin County?"

"Yes. I opened one here after leaving San Diego. Beautiful place, San Diego, but I needed a change of scenery, so came up north about ten years ago. Best move I ever made."

After reading Lawrence Brennan's rap sheet, I calculated his move was shortly after he pleaded guilty to forty felony counts in which he stole fifteen million dollars from seventy-five elderly clients. If he was the man I suspected, that move to Northern California occurred after his stint in a San Diego jail, and when he started a new investment business with an assumed name.

We finished our lamb curry, killed off the bottle of wine, and ordered three bowls of ice cream and coffee for the men. I didn't need caffeine for another sleepless night. Sam hadn't taken his eyes off Lloyd since we sat down, and I knew he was imprinting every detail of the man's face into his brilliant investigative mind.

After the goodbyes and "glad to meet you's" had been said, Lloyd took the elevator to his apartment, and I insisted Sam come to my place for a few minutes. No way was he leaving without telling me his impression of the so-called Lloyd Bellingham.

Chapter 33

"I have to make that drive to Oakland, you know," Sam said after refusing my offer of an after-dinner drink. He was sitting on the Lazy Boy with his feet up when, in an off-handed manner, he said, "No doubt in my mind, Lily. Your friend Lloyd is Lawrence Brennan, wanted fugitive. I'll be a hero at the Bureau when they hear I found their man."

I wanted to proclaim it was I, not Sam, who found one of the FBI's most wanted, but, at the moment, taking credit for Lloyd's downfall wasn't high on my achievement list.

"Don't you think we should wait until we find a motive for these murders?"

"The motive will become clear once he's in custody and the authorities start going through his bank fraud. Prosecuting him on murder charges will fall to the local authorities, anyway, as a first priority. Scams like your friend Lloyd committed are invariably complex, and prosecutors are so overburdened with these felonies that even when the perpetrators are caught, there are often long delays before the case goes to trial. The first order of business will be a preliminary hearing for the homicides."

Before Sam left, I gave him the baggie containing the white threads and told him, "You may want to give this to the DA. Before the trial, they can examine it for DNA."

"I'll get in touch with my friend at the FBI tomorrow and let them take over the investigation. They'll give the information to the local U.S. Attorney's office to investigate the murders. It will probably be a first in FBI history, discovering one of their Most Wanted has been hiding out in an old people's home."

He gave me a bear hug as he left and said, "I'll call you after I talk to Mallory and keep you in the loop. You did good work, Lily, and I'm proud of my little protégé."

I closed the door behind him.

After crawling beneath my down comforter, I got very little sleep. Images of Lloyd in an orange jumpsuit behind iron bars crowded my brain. I wiped them away with a vision of Monique strangled by her beautiful orange scarf.

Early the next morning, Lloyd called. His voice was icy cold, unlike anything I'd heard before. "Was last night intended to be an ambush?"

"What are you talking about?'

"You know what I'm talking about. Your friend, Sam, quizzed me like I was one of his slimy clients."

"He was being polite. What's your problem? A guilty conscious?"

"I don't like being set up, Lily"

"Look, Lloyd, I don't know what you're talking about. There was no so-called "setup." I simply thought you'd like to meet Sam. If you feel offended, I'm sorry."

"Well, I think we'd better discuss this further. I'll pick you up tonight for dinner. We can go out to Bodega Bay."

"It's not Friday night."

"No matter. I want to talk to you about a few things, and think we should do it away from this place."

There was no way in hell I was going anywhere with this psycho. Especially to a deserted area like Bodega Bay.

"Let me get back to you this afternoon. Right now, I'm leaving for my volunteer stint at City Hall. We can talk later about dinner."

After hanging up, I immediately called Sam and repeated my conversation with Lloyd.

"Don't worry, Lily. I've put in a call to the local police and by this evening, your friend will be tucked away in the Marin County Jail."

"Are you sure?"

"Absolutely. After hearing about the alias and his criminal past, the Attorney General's office is putting together an arrest warrant and it will be served sometime today. Stay away from him until then, Lily."

"Of course, I will. Thankfully, I'll be gone all day volunteering in the DA's office."

I was assigned to Joan's office that day, as she had a heavy workload of misdemeanors, including a public intoxication in Sausalito, as well as a petty theft case at an upscale women's store. I tried to stay focused on the work at hand, but my mind kept drifting to Journey's End. Would the authorities arrive today and put Lloyd in handcuffs?

I could only imagine what Dicky Davis was going through. Journey's End's reputation for being 'Retirement Living at Its Finest' would be forever tarnished when news about the arrest of one of its residents became known. I could see the headlines in the *San Francisco Chronicle* now: "Murderer and Scam Artist Found Hiding Out in Posh Marin Retirement Home."

When I returned to the Home after my volunteer stint, everything appeared normal. There were no police cars outside, no residents in the lobby gossiping about Lloyd's arrest, and after poking my head in Dicky's office, I discovered it was empty.

There was no one I could ask if anything out of the ordinary had happened during the day without arousing suspicion, so I rode the elevator to my apartment and waited. For what, I didn't know. Maybe a call from Sam, keeping me "in the loop" as he promised, or perhaps the one call Lloyd was allowed from the county jail.

After pouring myself a glass of wine, I stood at the window looking down at the vineyard. My feelings fluctuated between sadness and elation. Sadness for having been duped into thinking an evil man was my friend, as well as elation at knowing that I was part of his downfall.

Chapter 34

At nine o'clock the next morning, I received a call from Dick Davis, summoning me to his office.

"Come in, Lily, and sit down. I want you to be the first to know that Lloyd Bellingham was arrested yesterday. Four plainclothes police came to the building about noon. They had a warrant to search his apartment and to place him under arrest. They would only tell me that he was wanted for questioning in a police matter that they weren't free to discuss. I took them to Bellingham's apartment, and two cops stayed to search it. The other two took him out the back way to a waiting car. Whatever the reason for his being apprehended, this is not good for Journey's End's reputation."

How typical for Dicky to think only of his kingdom being under attack. I was tempted to tell him that things were only going to get worse, but he had already started interrogating me.

"I understand you and Mr. Bellingham were pretty

good friends. Do you have any idea what the police would want with him?"

Gloating over Lloyd's capture was the last thing on my mind, but I couldn't contain myself. "Remember when I told you the wheelchair deaths happening here this past year were more than accidents?"

"You're not insinuating Mr. Bellingham had anything to do with those deaths, are you?"

"So far there's no evidence, but once the FBI completes their investigation into his fraudulent investment business, I'm sure they'll find something that will connect him to our victims here."

"What fraudulent investment business?"

I found it very satisfying to tell Dicky a story based on proof and not conjecture or instinct. From the Public Records Search Service website findings to the FBI's identity confirmation, I related all the sins of Lloyd's past, including the alias name he used when taking up residency at Journey's End.

"Nice old man, right? Very kind. Very quiet. He came across as honest, but he had everyone fooled, especially me."

"Well, let's try and keep this unfortunate turn of events from the residents as long as possible. No doubt, the *Marin Independent Journal* will have a front-page story on the arrest by tomorrow. Meanwhile, it's best we don't stir the gossip pot."

Once again, I was repelled by Dicky's selfish concern about the Home's reputation. "Don't you think sending out a written statement to each resident with a vague comment about the arrest would help with speculation? Being a lawyer and all, I'm sure you can come up with some legalese that will soften the story."

"Good idea, Lily. I'll get right on it before the morning paper comes out."

Of course, Dicky's one-page, single-spaced announcement of Mr. Bellingham's arrest did little to quell the speculation and theories that took place with great gusto. At each meal, the bridge table, the tennis courts and wherever more than two people gathered, hushed conversations started or ended with the words "Bellingham" and "arrest."

The *Independent Journal*'s story mentioned only the financial scams; the murders were still under intense investigation and not a word was leaked to the press. But the front-page article was enough to disgorge some interesting tidbits from residents.

"I knew that guy from about five years ago when I was looking for an investment advisor," several reported, including Bob Wallace, who at one time was my prime suspect.

"Something about the guy didn't seem right. Lucky for me, I decided to handle my own investments," Wallace told anyone who would listen.

At my next volunteer stint with the DA's office, Lloyd's arrest was the hot topic. The entire staff was aware that I, too, lived at Journey's End and was eager to find out how well I knew him. Because Joe Pastori was close to filing charges, he avoided talking to me about the man arrested at my address. But Joan was eager to hear all I knew, and I was willing to tell her.

"Did you have a romantic relationship with him?" she asked after I mentioned our Friday night dinners.

"No, no. He had a hang-up of some sort about getting too involved with anyone. In retrospect, it was most likely due to fear of having his hidden past exposed."

"Why don't you ask him? He's being held in the county jail right next door, and I'll bet he'd like a visitor about now."

Why the hell would I visit that scumbag?

"Do you think that would be a good idea?"

"Sure. Since you and he were friends, he might tell you something helpful in the case against him. If you want, I can arrange a visit with the Sheriff's Department."

"Let me think about it, and I'll let you know."

Joan had no idea about the part I played in Bellingham's capture, but I knew, and it made me wonder if seeing the man again was a good idea. If I did visit, what the hell would I say? "Sorry, Lloyd, but I'm the one who unmasked you."

I spent the next few days mulling the idea over; I even

called Sam for his opinion. His answer was, as I suspected, "Do what you want."

On my next volunteer day, I told Joan that I'd appreciate her making a call to the Sheriff regarding a visit with Brennan, AKA Bellingham. She put the call on speakerphone.

"Oh, I remember Lily Lawrence," I heard him say. "I had a couple of meetings with that lady before this whole thing came down. Smart woman with some good instincts. Sure, tell her to come next Sunday. It's visitors day."

Chapter 35

I was a nervous wreck as I parked Rosie the following Sunday in a spot marked "Visitor," and walked to the entrance of the jail. At the front door, a deputy had me leave my over-sized handbag in a grey bin, along with my heavy parka. I tried to imagine he was a TSA employee and I was on my way to Hawaii.

After being escorted down a long hallway, I entered a room filled with tables and chairs bolted to the floor. I was told to take a seat and Mr. Brennan would be called shortly. I almost corrected the deputy. "Not Mr. Brennan. I'm here for Mr. Bellingham." It would take me a while to get comfortable with the name change.

Twenty minutes later, I saw the tall frame of my Friday night date enter the room. His balding head was lowered to the floor, and clad in the bright orange jump suit (definitely not his color); he looked like a man on his way to the gallows. He had aged ten years in the past two weeks, and for a fleeting moment, I felt a pang of sorrow.

"It's nice of you to visit," he said.

"I was asked to check up on your well-being," I lied. "Everyone at Journey's End is sure your arrest is some sort of mistake, and you'll be back at the Home in no time."

I felt compelled to say something nice because a small glimmer of hope still remained that the man who pushed my wheelchair and took me out to dinner was, in the depths of his soul, a decent person. Truth be told, Sam called during the week to say the FBI discovered additional damaging evidence. Seems as if Lloyd made financial investments for Marin County clients in recent years, despite the fact his license was revoked after the incarceration in San Diego.

"My attorney tells me otherwise. Seems as if I'm being charged with what I'm told were murders at the retirement home. Did you know anything about that, Lily?"

I wanted to tell him, "Yes" but instead, said, "I don't know much about the murders, but I'm told the FBI has you on their Most Wanted List for financial fraud against the elderly. And how do you explain hiding out for the last ten years under an assumed name?"

"Listen, Lily, there is a lot of truth in the fraud case the FBI has against me, but I want you to know I didn't start off as a thief. I bet even Bernie Madoff didn't. I was just trying to do the best I could for my clients. It's a cutthroat world out there. You make a bad trade. You lose some money. But you know you'll get it back. So you move some other money into that account. Just for a day, maybe a week. When the next trade comes in, you'll make it up and then some. It isn't stealing. In the end, your clients will be better off. You start small like that, a little crossing of the line, but then what can you do about it? If you admit what've you've done, you're ruined. You'll go to jail. Which is what happened to me down in San Diego.

"So what other choice did I have? You have to keep borrowing from Peter to pay Paul and hope that something will click, some Hail Mary pass will work, so you can get out from under."

I wished he left Peter, Paul and the Virgin Mary out of the conversation. It was blasphemous, and I found myself furious with this arrogant man for trying to justify the heartache he caused so many people.

"But you were caught for scamming previously. You went to jail, and after being a free man, went right back to cheating people. Bottom line, you steal from your clients, live a good life with all that stolen money, and are probably able to hire an expensive attorney."

"I'm still in jail. At the arraignment, the prosecutor read outlandish charges of homicide. I, of course, pled not guilty and was still denied bail. When the judge asked if I needed assistance from a court-appointed attorney, I had to say no and hire an expensive lawyer. Luckily, I have an old friend who is one of the finest criminal lawyers around."

How convenient he just happened to have a highly respected criminal attorney as an old friend, and probably an accomplice in the frauds.

I never heard Lloyd talk on and on. It was as if he'd been in solitary confinement for the past week.

"They've set a date for the preliminary hearing. I'm not worried because the prosecution can't possibly have enough evidence to meet its burden of proof for these so-called murders.

"Honest to God, Lily, I can't imagine where these charges stem from. Under the search warrant, the only things taken from my apartment were my white cashmere sweater and some files in the desk. But it basically doesn't matter, because if there's not enough evidence for the murders, I'll be facing the Feds for charges on the fraud. After they finish with me, my future doesn't look good."

Those were the first factual words I heard come out of Lloyd's mouth.

Maybe the man was actually facing reality. Realizing I had nothing more to say, I got up to leave. Thankfully, a voice from a loudspeaker in the ceiling bellowed out "Visiting hour is over." I breathed a sigh of relief and walked to the door.

"Thanks for coming, Lily," he called after me. "I hope to see you again soon."

Fat chance of that happening until I see you in court.

I walked out to fresh air, sunshine and freedom—all the splendors of life that Lawrence Brennan, aka Lloyd Bellingham, would never experience again in his lifetime.

Chapter 36

Sam promised he would attend Lloyd's preliminary hearing and call me when it was over.

"You would have been stunned," he told me that evening. "An indictment was presented and the prosecution is going for the death penalty. Pastori pointed out that the case involved multiple victims, a special circumstance that makes Brennan eligible for capital punishment. He also presented those pages from the datebook you found with the initials of each victim on the day they were killed.

"Since the prosecution had to only establish "probable cause" that a crime was committed, and the defendant is the culprit, it was a pretty low standard of proof to go to trial.

"I think the prosecution is waiting to hear additional info from the FBI on the fraud case, which will give them a connection to the murders. No doubt, there is enough evidence to proceed with a trial."

"When do you think a trial will start?"

"Could be as long as 12-15 months. Maybe more."

Wow, that's a long time for Lloyd to sit in a jail cell and think about the heinous crimes he committed. Then again, if he's convicted of the murders at Journey's End, he'll be in a prison cell for a hell of a lot longer.

I couldn't understand why I continued to feel sorry for a man who deceived so many for so long, not to mention taking four lives. Wheeling me to the dining room, the flowers, and, of course, those generous Friday night dinners away from the Home, hinted at some goodness in his heart. Or, was it all a fraud, like his business dealings? I should have remembered my father's advice, "Never judge a book by its cover."

After Lloyd's arrest and the gossip mill had run its course, Journey's End was more tedious than before. With no long hours combing the Internet for suspects, I had extra time to volunteer at the DA's office, which helped me escape the Home's dreariness. I also hoped to hear gossip about the State of California vs. Lawrence Brennan.

Sam stayed in touch with his friend at the FBI and, occasionally, checked in with the Sheriff's Department. "The wheels of justice move slowly, Lily," he warned me on more than one occasion. "Especially in a murder case where there's little evidence. Thanks to that thread you found, the sheriff's office is looking at the white sweater for comparison, but one piece of thread is not much to make even a circumstantial case. The strange notes in his datebook might hint at something, but the biggest hurdle for the prosecution is finding a motive for these killings. Jurors like to have a motive, especially when the victims are innocent senior citizens.

"Even though the guy had opportunity because of his proximity to the crime scenes, and, of course, the wheelchairs as the murder weapons, he pled "not guilty" at the arraignment. Who knows? Maybe he'll change his plea after the wheels of justice start moving."

I didn't want to think about what Sam was saying, and all this talk about murder weapons and crime scenes was giving me a headache.

"Don't tell me anymore until the trial begins," I finally said.

The wheels of justice didn't start moving until many, many months later. Finally, one day in early March of the next year, while working in Joe's office, I saw a trial schedule. His 'Inbox' held a pad of yellow lined paper, where he jotted down his schedule for the week. On page one, the name Lawrence Brennan appeared at the top, followed by April 1, 9:00 a.m., Courtroom 200, Judge Lucy S. Hemming presiding.

The Trial

Chapter 37

"How long do you think the trial will last?" I asked Sam when we met for lunch at Dolce Luna the last week of March.

"No telling. It could go on for as long as the prosecution needs to prove its case beyond a reasonable doubt. Personally, I'm afraid that's going to be hard to do with what they have to work with."

"You told me before that they have the weapons, the opportunity, the thread that matches his sweater, the datebook. If there is any of Brennan's DNA from the thread and sweater, isn't that positive evidence?"

"I suppose because people watch TV shows like *CSI* all the time, jurors put a lot of weight on scientific proof," Sam said. "Hopefully, the prosecutor will find something before the trial begins. If there is DNA on that piece of thread, it will be a good piece of evidence. Or, it could be useless, because the defense can argue that half the men in Marin County own white cashmere sweaters.

"If it's any consolation, there's no question the FBI have him for the fraud, so if he does get away with murder, he'll still be spending a long, long time in a federal prison."

"That's not enough. I want him found guilty of Monique's murder, and I'm going to be in that courtroom every day of the trial."

"You may not be allowed if you're called as a witness. "

"Me? A witness?"

"Who knew him best in the past year, and who found the incriminating thread, the datebook, his booking mug on the Internet site? You, Lily. So think of yourself as a prime witness for the prosecution."

Holy Shit! It hadn't crossed my mind that I could be called to testify at the trial. The thought of it made me physically ill. But if I were subpoenaed, I would do it for Monique.

The day before the trial was to begin, Joe Pastori served me with a subpoena to appear as a witness. Jury selection started the next day. Sam attended the two days it took to select the twelve jurors and two alternates, while I waited, counting on him to update me on what transpired. With jury selection completed, we met for dinner and he gave me a detailed account.

"This is like the good old days when I was a major player in the courtroom," he told me. I caught the excitement in his voice.

"There must have been over a hundred potential jurors waiting in the courtroom when the court clerk, dressed like a typical paper pusher in a brown tweed suit, paisley bow tie and horn-rimmed glasses, announced Judge Hemming as the presiding judge.

"Lucy Hemming is a tall, attractive woman with graying hair and a pleasant face. She's also a very fair judge. She told the jury their sole responsibility would be to judge guilty or not guilty, and not concern themselves with the penalty or punishment phase. Then, she asked the most important question in a trial, "Do you all agree innocent until proven guilty?

"Of course, they all shook their heads 'yes' and then, Lily, the hours dragged on. The aged, deaf and sick were excused, as well as those the Judge deemed had a legitimate excuse. The jury pool was asked a load of questions by the judge before noon, and when everyone returned from lunch, the lawyers got their shot at the remaining people. Finally, the attorneys started the voir dire."

"What's that?"

"It's when the attorney uses his gut instincts to accept or reject a juror."

"What an ordeal. So do they finally have a jury?"

"Yep—five men and seven women, ranging from an engineer to a housewife to a couple of retirees. After Judge Hemming warned them not to talk to anyone about the case while the trial was ongoing, they were dismissed for the day, and told to return the next morning at 9:00 a.m. sharp. That's when Joe Pastori will give his opening remarks."

Since I was scheduled to be a witness in Joe's case, I was banished from my volunteer job until the trial was over. "Just as a precaution," Joan told me.

Chapter 38

"Joe's opening was strong and forceful," Sam told me on the first day of trial. "The defense's statement was only so-so."

His prejudice was showing, but who was I to argue?

After opening statements, the prosecutor started off with his first witness—ME. I couldn't believe it when I was told to be in the courtroom the next morning at 9 o'clock.

"No one has even given me a practice session like they do on TV," I moaned to Sam after receiving my notice to appear the next day.

"Pastori thought it best if you just get on the stand and answer his questions truthfully and to the best of your ability."

"Of course, I'll do that. But a short rehearsal wouldn't hurt."

"Listen to me, Lily. If you tell the truth and tell it accurately, the defense can't cross you up, and if you don't know an answer to any question, it's best to say, 'I don't know' or 'I don't remember.'

"Dress conservatively. No tee shirts with obscene symbols, and no flashy jewelry."

"I don't own tee shirts with obscene symbols anymore, and I never owned flashy jewelry."

"And don't forget to answer the questions, 'Yes sir' and 'No sir,' even to Pastori, who you usually call "Joe." And, of course, always address the judge as 'your Honor.'

"Will you quit treating me like a five-year-old who has no manners?"

"Also, be attentive. Remain alert at all times so you can hear and understand the question. And, most importantly, answer all the questions directly. I know how you like to ramble, ad lib, or crack a joke, and how you get under pressure. Any wisecracking will make it look as if you aren't taking your role seriously."

"Are you kidding? This is probably the most serious role I've played since my third marriage."

"If it's any comfort, I don't think you'll be on the stand long. Probably for just a question or two regarding finding Mrs. Wilson's body, searching the bushes for that piece of thread and going through the datebook. Can you handle that?"

"Sure. I'll just tell my story the way it happened."

"By the way, why don't you wear that nice navy blue

suit you had when you worked for me? It's conservative and sincere looking—perfect for a witness."

"Sorry, Sam, but I outgrew that suit four years ago. Don't worry, I won't embarrass you."

But at bedtime, that was one of my many worries. Would I screw up on the stand and not only ruin the case for Joe, but embarrass my old boss by making an ass of myself? With those thoughts whirling through my brain, I dropped off to sleep after swallowing a couple of Advil PM's.

I slept like a rock, almost missing the alarm going off at seven o'clock. After showering, I put on the black dress I usually wore to funerals at the Home, and took off in the Mini for my big day in court. If everyone stuck to the script, I knew exactly how to answer their questions. I'd repeat my story of finding Mrs. Wilson the same way I'd told Dicky and Nurse Ratched, and relate my search of the thread and Lloyd's apartment in the most truthful way I knew how.

My ride to the courthouse took less than fifteen minutes, but it felt like an eternity. I just wanted to get the ordeal behind me. Sam was in the lobby to escort me to the hallway outside Judge Hemming's courtroom, where we sat for half-an-hour until both attorneys finished their various motions before the jury filed in. When the jury was seated, the attorneys returned to their respective tables. After it was confirmed the accused, Lawrence Brennan, was present, Joe Pastori announced his first witness for the prosecution—Lily Lawrence.

Chapter 39

I entered the courtroom as Joe took his place at the dais. My legs shook like a seven point earthquake, and my stomach rumbled with its aftershocks.

Joe greeted the jury and said, "I'd like to call my first witness, Lily Lawrence."

I hurried up the aisle. I wasn't worried about Joe, as I knew he would be kind. It was cross-examination by David Black that worried me. From episodes I'd watched of *Law and Order* through the years, the defense lawyers were always biting, sarcastic, mean adversaries.

The clerk swore me in, and I tried to not trip on my high heels as I slid into the witness box. "Good morning, Ms. Lawrence."

"Good morning, Mr. Pastori."

How weird. I'd known this man for over six months, always called him 'Joe,' and had even shared a lunch or two with him. Now, he was like a stranger.

"Can you give your full name and address for the court reporter," Joe asked as if he'd never met me.

"My name is Lily Lawrence, L-a-w-r-e-n-c-e. I live at the Journey's End Retirement Home at 85 Valley Oaks Drive in San Rafael, California."

"Inasmuch as the defendant lived at that address until his arrest, I assume you met Lawrence Brennan at that time."

"Yes. Except I knew him as Lloyd Bellingham."

There was an objection from Mr. Black and Judge Hemming instructed me that I was to answer simply 'yes' or 'no'.

"Yes."

I haven't been up here five minutes, and already I have the ire of the judge.

"Did you get to know him well?"

"I thought so."

Again there is an objection from Black, but Judge Hemming ignored it.

"Can you give us the circumstances of your friendship with the defendant?"

I started from the beginning with his assistance while I was stuck in a wheelchair for several months, and moved on to our Friday night dinner dates.

"Was this a romantic relationship?"

"Oh no. Far from it. Just two residents escaping the confines of a retirement home one night a week."

I expected Mr. Black to object, but he was quietly sitting at the defense table scribbling on a yellow pad with a Mont Blanc pen.

"Now, I would like you to tell the jury about finding Mrs. Wilson's body at Journey's End."

This part was easy inasmuch as I'd told the story over and over again since it happened two years previously. Starting with my walk around the Promenade, I repeated the events etched in my mind.

"After finding Mrs. Wilson's body, did you ever return to the scene of her accident?"

He knew damn well I had because I was questioned repeatedly about my finding the white thread, which was the sole reason I was sitting in this witness chair.

"Yes."

"And when was that, Ms. Lawrence?"

"The first time was when I showed Mr. Davis, Journey's End CEO, where I found Mrs. Wilson's body. Then, several months later, I returned to search through the bushes in the event her killer had left some sort of clue."

"Why did you assume she had been killed when the Marin County coroner ruled her death an accident?"

"Having worked for a private investigator many years

before my retirement, I learned to question unusual deaths, and considered the place and manner of Mrs. Wilson's death very unusual. That is why I went back to the bushes to look for signs of foul play."

"And did you find anything in those bushes?"

"Yes. I found a thin white cashmere thread."

Joe walked to the prosecution table and picked up two bags. A large one held the sweater taken from Lloyd's armoire during the warrant search, and a smaller bag held the single white thread.

"Do you recognize these items?'

"Yes. The sweater belongs to the defendant and the thread is the one I found in the bushes."

"How do you know the sweater belongs to the defendant?'

"Because he wore it one evening when I had him over for dinner."

"And when did you discover these datebook pages?" he asked handing me a plastic bag with the pages I'd copied from Lloyd's datebook.

"When I went to his apartment to water plants while he was out of town. He'd given me his keys so I could go up a couple times in his absence. I'd forgotten the date of his return home, and when rifling through his calendar to confirm when I could stop watering the plants, I happened to see those particular pages. I thought the notations on the days of the murders were strange and might be of importance."

I dared to look down at the defense table and into Lloyd's eyes. Thank God, looks don't really kill.

Chapter 40

"That is all, Ms. Lawrence. Thanks for your cooperation." Judge Hemming addressed David Black. "Would the defense like to cross-examine?"

"No, your Honor, but I stipulate that the datebook pages found in Mr. Brennan's apartment be expunged as evidence, as they were taken without a warrant."

With that, Judge Hemming called both attorneys to the bench for a whispered conversation before addressing the jury. "I will give my decision on the presentation of specific evidence at a later time. You may step down, Ms. Lawrence."

I couldn't believe the ordeal was over so quickly. Expecting to be attacked like a hungry lion by the defense, I didn't know whether to feel relieved or insulted that I was let off so easy. Was my testimony so insignificant? And what was the big deal with the datebook I'd found? The prosecution thought it was a significant piece of evidence, and had no qualms over the manner in which I'd found it.

After all, I did have a key and permission to enter Lloyd's apartment. There was no law barring a nosy broad from looking around. Obviously, the defense didn't see it that way, but we would have to wait for the judge to rule. For now, I was free to join Sam in the back row as an observer for the duration of the trial.

Joe's next witness, Ms. Weil, was a technician from the Marin County crime lab. A middle-aged woman with an intelligent, kind face, she reminded me of my third grade teacher, Sister Magdalene at St. Cecilia's School. After being sworn in, she began a litany of her credentials, years working for the county, and scientific background.

Finally, Joe asked, "As an employee of the Marin County CSI unit, what was your assignment in the present case?"

"I was given a white sweater to compare with a single thread, as well as a silk scarf and motorized wheel chair used by one of the victims."

Sam looked at me with wide-eyed surprise. "Did you know anything about the prosecution looking at Monique's chair?" he whispered.

"Someone from the sheriff's office called Dicky Davis a couple months ago and asked if any personal items belonging to the victims might still be at Journey's End. He called me because of my friendship with Monique and

I told him that I had the orange scarf and her scooter was in my storage bin. I hated giving them up, but I realized it was to look for DNA against Lloyd. And what do you know? DNA doesn't lie," I whispered back.

"Did you find anything on these items, Ms. Weil?"

"I wasn't able to find usable DNA on the wool thread, inasmuch as it had been placed in a plastic bag prior to testing. Plastic bags do not breathe, and can cause moisture and mold to grow on fabric, which in turn can have a negative effect on DNA testing. In addition, the thread was exposed to the elements for several months, thus destroying any usable sample. I did, however, match the single thread to the sweater. The fibers were a definite match."

"And did you examine the motorized scooter?"

"Yes. I dusted for fingerprints and came up with a number of them. Some, of course, belonged to the victim, others matched Lily Lawrence, and there was one large palm print. After running it through AFIS, the Automated Fingerprint Identification System, I found a match to the defendant."

Holy Shit! I felt terrible I had put the thread in a baggie, thus destroying DNA, but how was I to know? Plastic bags were never discussed on *CSI*. The good news was that she was able to match the thread to Lloyd's sweater, and there was Lloyd's palm print on the wheelchair.

During the break, Sam was elated. "This case is looking

better and better for the prosecution," he said. "Let's see how the defense explains away the scientific evidence."

Even I, with all my negative proclivities, was seeing a shining light at the end of this long dark tunnel.

Chapter 41

As anticipated, Mr. Black immediately disputed the technician's findings on his cross-examination, accusing her of sloppy, misguided work, and tainted evidence. But as an experienced prosecution witness, Ms. Weil was more than able to hold her own.

The prosecution's follow-up witnesses were people related to the victims. I had never gotten around to calling relatives or friends of Mrs. Wilson or Mrs. Shaw, but, apparently, Joe Pastori's office had found several. And they were all here to tell a horror story of financial ruin suffered by the victims.

Rosalie Ryan and her husband, Gordon, had been friends of Mrs. Wilson through their many years in the insurance business. The court clerk swore in Gordon Ryan.

"How did you become acquainted with Mrs. Wilson?' Joe asked him.

"Her husband and I became good friends through

business dealings, and, upon his death, my wife and I continued the friendship."

"During these years, did Mrs. Wilson ever come to you for financial advice?"

"Only once, and it was very disturbing."

"In what way?"

"Well, I knew she and her husband built their lives, brick by brick, on a foundation of hope, hard work, and devotion to each other. When Mr. Wilson passed away, Shirley took the reins and continued to keep their thriving business as lucrative and successful as her husband. But just before moving to the Journey's End, she wanted to increase her assets for the expenses that awaited her in retirement, so she contacted this Lloyd Bellingham, a financial advisor in San Rafael. He vowed to take care of her as long as she lived."

"So what was the problem?"

"The problem was that he single-handedly almost destroyed Mrs. Wilson's life by investing her money, about $600,000, in real estate deals. He told her the money was safe and would earn a steady monthly return of 8 to 12 percent. Then, the housing bubble burst, and so did the monthly income. As far as I know, she never recouped any of it."

"Why didn't she go to the authorities?"

"First, it was shame that a smart businesswoman like

herself could be scammed in such a way, and then the stroke came along. At that point, she was too sick and feeble to think of anything but getting back on her feet, so we never discussed it again."

"Thank you, Mr. Ryan. You are excused."

Mr. Black had objected throughout Ryan's testimony that it was immaterial to the case, but Judge Hemming dismissed his objections at every turn.

Of course it was relevant to the case. It was motive for the killing.

The next witness had been summoned from England to tell of Mrs. Shaw's distress over a goodly sum of money she'd invested in an annuity after attending a two-hour sales seminar sponsored by financial advisor, Lloyd Bellingham.

"The man told her it was like a CD—safe and guaranteed. He never mentioned the term of the annuity must be less than or equal to her life expectancy, and the total payments must be greater than the amount invested. Of course, she didn't understand any of this, didn't meet the parameters, and consequently lost her entire investment with no recourse against the scoundrel who sold it to her."

A pattern was beginning to emerge for motive, and I wondered if Jacques would be coming from France to relate a tragic financial situation Monique had been suckered into.

Chapter 42

That Friday evening, I received a call from Jacques Marquise. He was calling from a local motel to invite me to dinner on Saturday night. Of course, I was delighted not only to hear from him, but to know he would be testifying on behalf of Monique and putting another nail in Lloyd's coffin.

We agreed to meet at a fancy French restaurant in Larkspur at 8 p.m. Accustomed to eating dinner by six and being in bed by ten, I wasn't sure if I could stave off my hunger until eight, but I told myself that it was a small sacrifice compared to what Jacques had endured to make this trip.

I arrived at the restaurant early, and took a table near the front door. At five minutes past eight, Jacques walked in and was hard to miss. A dark beret was angled on his head, and he had an ascot tied around his neck. Even in a county that had its share of eccentrics, he certainly made a statement. I was ashamed at my embarrassment when he shouted my name and came to the table. He leaned over and gave me one of those airy, European kisses.

"It is so nice to see you, Mademoiselle Lawrence, even under these unfortunate circumstances."

Regardless of his attire, I greeted him warmly. His pretension continued when he sprinkled a French word here and there as he gave our food and drink order to the waitress.

Waiting for our expensive French wine to arrive, I said, "It's wonderful you were able to come and testify for the prosecution."

"How could I refuse? I now have the opportunity to help right the wrong my dear Monique suffered at the hands of that terrible man."

"Before we get into conversation about the trial, Jacques, I think someone told me to not talk about testimony before it's given in court. So to be on the safe side, let's not discuss what you're going to say tomorrow. I wouldn't want us to have your testimony thrown out because we broke some sort of rule."

"Oui, I understand. We will simply talk about life and, as you Americans say, we can always talk about the weather."

But we didn't talk about the weather, because Jacques easily took over the conversation in his heavy French accent telling me about his many dalliances with the beautiful women who populated Paris.

His stories were sexy and certainly nothing like anything I'd heard for the past twenty years, so the time flew by, and it was soon ten o'clock. My inner clock cried out "bedtime," so I suggested we talk again tomorrow when Jacques was finished in court.

"Oui. I hope to be instrumental in putting this Lawrence Brennan behind bars."

"I'm sure your testimony will be a big help, Jacques, but you should also enjoy your time in the Bay Area. There's a ferryboat that leaves from here in Larkspur that will bring you to San Francisco's waterfront. Once there, you can find all kinds of transportation to get around the city."

I suspected he wanted me to offer a tour or some such thing, but I wasn't in the mood to escort a man, even a sexy Frenchman, around the city. At the restaurant's door, we exchanged the airy kisses once again, and he said, "Au revoir."

Driving home, I hoped Joe could get the jury to understand Jacques' damaging words without an interpreter.

The weekend dragged along until court was to reconvene on Monday. I did laundry, read the Sunday paper with its front-page story on Lloyd's trial (I still couldn't call him "Lawrence Brennan"), and ended Sunday night watching a re-run of *Law and Order.* Monday would bring the television show to reality.

Chapter 43

Joe Pastori arranged for a car to pick Jacques up at his motel and had someone escort him to Courtroom 200. With a ride and escort, it was assumed that when the trial commenced at 9 a.m., Jacques would be on the stand.

But before court proceedings started for the day, there was a forty-five minute postponement. The defense requested a meeting in the judge's chambers to discuss admittance of the datebook pages I'd found in Brennan's apartment. Sam and I, and a courtroom of spectators, waited and fidgeted in our seats. Jacques, I imagined, was pacing in the hallway, confused about the delay.

Finally at 9:45, we all stood when Judge Hemming entered the room followed by two solemn looking attorneys. David Black's face told it all. The defense lost its appeal. Judge Hemming allowed the pages entered as evidence, explaining to the jury that the pages were obtained after permission was given to enter the apartment. Anything found while there was legally obtained.

"You may consider notations in the datebook while deliberating the verdict," she said. "Now, Mr. Pastori, you may call your next witness."

"Chalk up another victory for you," Joe whispered.

Jacques was summoned from the hall, and took the stand. Thank God, the beret and ascot were gone and he looked like a Wall Street banker in his perfectly tailored navy suit, white shirt, blue striped tie and shiny, black, pointed-toe shoes.

"Mr. Marquise, I understand you are the cousin of one of the victims, Monique Marquise," Joe said, standing very near the witness box.

"Oui, I am her only living relative."

"And you reside in Paris, France?"

"Oui."

Suddenly, Black was out of his chair.

"I object to this man's use of a foreign language while testifying, and I ask your Honor to instruct the witness to use the word 'yes' instead of 'oui.'"

Picky, picky. Obviously, David Black was still stinging from Judge Hemming's ruling against him on the datebook page issue.

"Mr. Marquise, the court requests that you refrain from answering in your language and use the word 'yes' or 'no.' I assume you are capable of that?"

"Oui, your Honor."

She smiled broadly and told Pastori to continue his examination.

"Were you in regular contact with your cousin after her move to Journey's End?"

"Yes. We talked at least twice a month."

"And did she ever mention a man named Lawrence Brennan?"

"A few weeks before her death, Monique called to tell me a story she said I wouldn't believe."

"And what was that?

"A man named Lawrence Brennan, who had cheated her on an investment she'd made before moving into the retirement home, was living in her building. She was afraid to confront him or call the authorities. I asked if there was anyone she could confide in before contacting the police. She was hesitant about involving her close friend, Lily Lawrence, but said there was a very bright, elderly gentleman who knew many influential people in the area. She thought he might help."

"Did she give you the elderly man's name?"

"Rosenberg, Rothenberg, something like that. I don't remember his name exactly, but she said he had been a well-known heart surgeon."

I let out a gasp as the entire scenario appeared before me. Like one of those giant jigsaw puzzles, all the pieces finally fell into place.

"After that conversation, did you and Monique talk again?"

"About a week later, she called and sounded calmer. She had talked to this nice doctor and he was going to call someone high up in your justice system. That was the last time we spoke."

"Thank you, Mr. Marquise, for coming from a long distance to testify. You may step down."

"You put that salaud away forever!" Jacques shouted as he stepped out of the witness box.

"Did he say "salad?' I whispered to Sam.

"Nah. I think it means "bastard" in French."

Chapter 44

No relatives or friends were called on Dr. Irv's behalf because Jacques' testimony had established a motive for the killing. With little fanfare, Joe addressed the court and said, "The prosecution rests."

My mind sifted through each testimony and I saw a pattern evolve exactly as I imagined. The fear of having his identity disclosed by one of his victims was more than Lloyd could accept. Disgrace and a long jail sentence in a federal prison were not on his bucket list of things to do before he died. Looking back on Lloyd Bellingham's kind, shy, quiet manner, it was still hard to imagine that beneath this veneer was a rotten, evil man.

The prosecution rested its case on a Friday afternoon, which left another long weekend to ponder what might come next. Would David Black attempt a defense? Would Lloyd testify? Could there possibly be any rebuttal to the evidence and testimony made against him? In my mind, the answer was "no." But, as Sam continued to remind me, one never knew what jurors were thinking when the death penalty was a factor.

Luckily, I had made plans to visit a friend in Los Angeles for the weekend, so Friday night I caught a late flight into LAX. Sherry and I met when my last husband and I lived in Southern California shortly before his death, and we kept in contact by e-mail and phone. Twice a year, I flew down for a visit, as some of my fondest memories are of good times spent in the beach town where Sherry lived. She was a retired teacher, divorced mother of two grown sons, and, at sixty-five, was always ready and eager to enjoy life. And enjoy life we did for two glorious days.

After sleeping late, we took our daily walk under bright blue skies on the sandy beach near her home, stopping at the local coffee house for a late breakfast and spending the remaining morning at many boutiques in her small town. With sore feet and numerous shopping bags, we returned to her house for a nap before dinner and fun at her favorite bistro.

Our conversations consisted mainly of the case against Lawrence Brennan, aka Lloyd Bellingham, who she'd become familiar with via my e-mails during the year of Friday night dinners. I found my mindset changing while telling Sherry details of the trial. Sentimentality no longer clouded my judgment and, from a distance, I saw the accused for what he was—a felonious fraud who killed four innocent old people to protect his sorry ass. I had been crushed to learn the truth about the man I considered a friend, and yet—this is going to sound odd—it was okay. In the end, the ugly truth is better than the prettiest of lies.

I also made a huge decision in those two days. When the trial was over and this sordid mess came to an end, I would leave Journey's End, return to Southern California and take an apartment near Sherry. Life didn't have to end for me at the Home. I had another twenty good years to live out.

Dreading my return home, I said a sad goodbye to Sherry before boarding my six p.m. flight back to SFO.

"I'll send an e-mail when the trial is over to let you know how it played out," I told her. "Meanwhile, keep an eye out for an apartment I might like. Preferably, somewhere near you so we can play together."

Chapter 45

Judge Hemming addressed Mr. Black when the trial resumed Monday morning. "Is the defense prepared to call its witnesses?"

"Your Honor, the defense will present its case in closing arguments."

There were murmurs throughout the courtroom. Everyone had been caught off guard by his pronouncement.

"Alright, then. Mr. Pastori, you may begin your closing argument."

Joe, dressed in his best suit, shiny black shoes, and sporting freshly cut hair, looked like a man who knew he would be center stage this morning before twelve jurors. His entire appearance was confident and self-assured when he walked to the dais and began to speak.

"Ladies and gentlemen of the jury, I want to thank each of you for your time and patience. I know the details of these horrendous crimes have been difficult as you envisioned your elderly mother, father or grandparents subjected to the malicious deeds of this defendant.

"Shirley Wilson, Edna Shaw, Monique Marquise and Dr. Irving Rosenberg did not deserve to die, and finding the defendant not guilty of murder would be condoning his uncontrolled anger for fear of being exposed for his financial misdeeds. These innocent people were living out their final years in a safe, peaceful retirement home. It was an environment designed to treat them with the respect and dignity earned after a lifetime of living by a moral code we've all been taught. And then, Lawrence Brennan entered their lives. First, ruining the financial security they had worked hard to attain, and, then, ending their lives. You've heard from friends and family members who testified to the financial damage he inflicted on these victims. And when he found himself living in the same facility as these people, he had to save himself from being exposed as the man who stole their money and walked away.

"Murder cases need to prove opportunity, motive and evidence. We have proposed that Mr. Brennan had all three. While in close proximity to Mrs. Wilson, Mrs. Shaw, Monique Marquise and Dr. Irving Rosenberg, he had easy opportunity. Witnesses have testified to his motive—fear of being reported to the authorities—and our crime lab has presented hard scientific evidence.

"Whose palm print was found on the very chair Ms. Marquise sat in when strangled by her scarf? Who owned a sweater matching a single thread found in the bushes where Shirley Wilson was murdered? And who made notes in a datebook to record his heinous deeds? All the evidence will prove to you that Mr. Brennan is the one, the only one, guilty of killing these innocent victims.

"You will not see anything in the jury instructions regarding insanity or senility, for it is not a defense. You should only see someone who fleeced these elderly people from their retirement money, and killed them to ensure no one would report him to the authorities.

"Keep in mind that these murders were unlawful killings with malice aforethought, along with proof beyond a reasonable doubt. The cloak has been pulled off the defendant through the evidence presented. He has been shown guilty and any doubt must be articulated, as it cannot be just a hunch or a feeling. Malice aforethought is a plan to act. Actions speak louder than words.

"He is guilty of first degree murder with premeditation. His actions were taken in a state of anger and self-preservation. For the sake of justice, I ask you to find this man, Lawrence Brennan, guilty of first-degree murder.

"Thank you."

I watched the jurors while Joe spoke, and saw only one elderly woman with tears in her sad, rheumy eyes.

Judge Hemming called for a ten-minute recess. Sam and I wandered out to the hallway, grabbed a coffee from the vending machine, and sat on a hard bench.

I don't know what Sam was thinking but my thoughts kept drifting to the grotesque sight of a seventy-three year old man lying on a gurney with a deadly needle in his arm. Then again, considering the rate at which California carried out the death penalty, Brennan would probably be closer to ninety-three.

When we returned to the courtroom after a forty-minute delay, Judge Hemming entered the courtroom. A long silence ensued as she rifled through papers and checked her laptop computer. Finally, she looked up and said, "The defense would like to make a statement."

It was not the closing argument we expected.

David Black stood and said, "Your Honor, my defendant would like to change his plea to "guilty," and accepts the prosecution's offer of life in prison without parole."

I heard a gasp in the courtroom. What happened in the past forty minutes to bring about this sudden change? Was it Joe's closing argument, or had Brennan finally seen the writing on the wall? I looked to Sam for an answer and he mouthed, "I'm not surprised."

In retrospect, it made sense. Brennan was headed to prison anyway once the FBI got their hands on him, so why chance a death sentence? His attorney had presented no defense, and the evidence he thought wasn't there, was actually stacked against him.

Judge Hemming instructed the defendant and attorneys to appear in her courtroom two weeks later for formal sentencing. She thanked the jury for their participation, and abruptly adjourned for the day.

There would be no additional witnesses, no closing defense arguments, and no waiting for a jury to decide the fate of Lawrence Brennan. He'd eliminated the remaining ritual by declaring his guilt in the murders at Journey's End, and there was no uncertainty about his future. For the rest of his life, he would call San Quentin home.

Sam and I headed to a nearby bar for a drink. We sat in a corner booth and hashed over the case, from the day I found Mrs. Wilson's body in the rhododendron bushes to the confession of guilt.

"Why do you think Brennan changed his plea without mounting any sort of defense?" I asked Sam sipping my second Stoli on the rocks.

"Easy. His attorney had no defense. If Brennan hadn't murdered those four people, who else was responsible? Hell, Lily, think back to when you first told me and anyone else who'd listen that these deaths were not accidents? No one believed you, including me, right? But who persisted—poking around for clues, wearing out the welcome mat at Deputy Thompson's office, and spending hours on the computer?

"From the start, I thought there wasn't a thread of evidence. Oh excuse me, you did have one thread, but, at that point, any conviction was a long shot. Then you found the datebook, and kept the scooter for possible clues. Hell, Lily, you're good enough to be a homicide detective."

"And who did I learn my sleuthing techniques from, huh? This conversation is like the good old days after we solved a case, but I don't deserve all the credit. You had your FBI contacts, and Joe did a hell of a job prosecuting. But you're right. We still have fire in our belly for justice. What do you say we reactivate the Levine Private Investigative office? Of course, we have to change the name to "Levine & Lawrence, P.I.'s. Has a nice alliterative ring to it."

I'd been thinking of my proposal for the past several weeks, but didn't want to distract our attention from Brennan's case. Discovering the Journey's End killer gave me something I hadn't felt since retiring—satisfaction and confidence I was still a contributor to society. Now, vocalizing my idea to Sam stirred up heightened enthusiasm for embarking on a new chapter in my aging years.

Chapter 46

We sat in silence for several minutes and I waited Sam out. He showed no reaction to my proposal so I tried another approach—flattery.

"Who would have thought one day you'd find your home invaders and Rebecca's killer in Mexico? You put both men behind bars after the police got nowhere in years. That goes to show that, even while on vacation and enjoying Rosa's assets, you still have what it takes."

"I don't know, Lily. Much as I hate to admit it, don't you think we're a little long in the tooth to be chasing felons? It's an interesting idea, but I want to bask in my laurels and maybe take up golf."

"Sam, we may not be the young hotshots we were twenty years ago, but I know Lily Lawrence, a seventy-year-old retiree, helped convict a man responsible for killing four people at a retirement home. The satisfaction I felt from giving some peace to all the people who'd been hurt, physically, financially and emotionally is a feeling I want to experience again."

"I know where you're coming from, but I need some time to mull over the idea. Besides, there will be a lot of logistics to figure out."

"Don't wait too long because my friend, Sherry, in Huntington Beach, is looking at a condo for me to buy. I have to get out of Journey's End, and thought maybe I might move back to Southern California. But if you go along with my idea, I'll look for a place to buy in Oakland, instead."

After our second drink, Sam reminded me he had a long drive across the bridge. "I wouldn't want to get picked up on a DUI, especially when we might be starting an investigative business. Wouldn't look good on our application. After Brennan is carted off to San Quentin, we can have another celebration. Hell, maybe, and I said maybe, we can combine it with the grand opening of Levine & Lawrence, PI's."

We walked to the parking lot, said we'd talk in a few days, and I drove off to Journey's End. Throughout the trial, I kept a low profile at the Home, often leaving by 8:30 in the morning to get a seat in the courtroom, and arriving to my apartment after 5 o'clock when everyone was at dinner. My profile was so low for the past week and a half that I missed any gossip permeating the walls of the building. Even Dicky had left me alone. Did any of them know the extent of my involvement in the case? I hoped not. But it was over, and time to emerge from my isolation to face the crowd of curious faces.

It turned out everyone at Journey's End was aware of my involvement with the murderer who'd been sent to prison for life. But all they knew, for a fact, was what they read in the daily paper. The news coverage had been extensive, because, as a crime reporter for the *Independent Journal* wrote, "How often does one hear of a serial killer living in an exclusive retirement home?"

I parked the Mini between the garbage cans, reminding myself I would soon be free of this and other aggravations. It was way past dinnertime when I entered my condo, and with two hefty drinks and a bowl of pretzels under my belt, I had little appetite. A can of soup, a glass of milk and an early bedtime seemed like a good idea. I wasn't even in the mood for *Law and Order, Criminal Minds* or *CSI*. In fact, I might lay off those shows for a very long time.

Chapter 47

At nine o'clock the next morning, my phone rang. It was Dicky Davis, asking if I would drop by his office sometime during the day. We agreed to one o'clock after he returned from lunch. I went back to sleep.

I'd once read that stress could be more tiring than physical labor, but had never experienced anything like the events of the past year. The emotional roller-coaster ride of the trial hadn't eased my anxieties, so it was no wonder my weary body finally caught up with my restless mind. Unsavory cases with elements of major crimes and felonies were part of my job when working for Sam, but were never on a personal level. These murders had taken over my heart and soul.

After waking again at ten o'clock, I made coffee, carried my cup to the small deck, sat down and opened the morning paper.

The front-page story in bold print headlines read: "Serial Killer at Retirement Home Pleads Guilty to Murders."

There was also a sketch of Brennan in his orange jump suit standing beside David Black at the defense table. The artist had portrayed Black looking more distraught than the man who just confessed to four vicious murders.

The article contained a date for sentencing—four weeks from today. At that time, Lawrence Brennan would recite his confession before Judge Hemming and she would hand down his sentence—life in prison with no chance of parole. The reporter hinted that the court might be lenient due to his age, but the hint was merely conjecture.

After a shower and shampoo, I dressed in jeans and a sweater, called Joan at the county offices and asked if I could come back to work

"You bet," she said. "We've missed you and the work has been piling up. How about tomorrow at ten o'clock?

"Great. See you then."

My stomach grumbled and I realized, like it or not, I should find some food in the dining room. My cupboard was bare and I needed to face the residents of Journey's End sometime.

As it turned out, I hadn't been missed. Having previously spent little time in the Home's dining room, people assumed that after testifying at the murder trial, I was being more hermit-like than usual. When I walked into the dining hall, there were a few curious glances and a couple hellos. One resident said, "Good to see you." Others didn't bother to look up from their walkers or wheelchairs. Unless reading the local paper was on their daily agenda, the disgrace of Lloyd Bellingham held little interest in their isolated lives.

I sat at a table with two new residents who did read the newspaper, for they proceeded to rehash the entire downfall of the former resident they never met. Some of their knowledge, based on rumors heard at the Home, was wrong, but I nodded my head, threw in a few tut-tuts, and feigned interest in their comments.

After finishing my sandwich, salad and tea, I went directly to Dicky's office. It was exactly one o'clock and he was nowhere to be found. His secretary said he'd left later than usual for lunch, but I could take a seat and wait. *Typical of his arrogance and over-blown ego to keep me waiting.*

At one-thirty, Davis arrived at his office. He actually apologized, telling me he had a radio interview to be aired at six tonight on a local station. Of course, it was regarding the conviction of Lawrence Brennan, and after being told the name of the station, I made a mental note to refrain from listening to KGO that evening.

My invitation to Dicky's office was an interrogation. He wanted to know every detail not already exposed in the media--particularly my participation in the trial.

"I really don't know any more than what you've read in the papers and seen on TV," I lied.

Feeling unrestrained from any niceties, I said, "You do realize, Dick, none of this would have happened if you vetted incoming residents more thoroughly, and believed me when I said Mrs. Wilson's death was not an accident."

"Are you trying to blame me for the deaths that occurred here?"

"No. But if you'd researched Brennan's past, I'm sure the Admittance Committee would never have approved his residency and Journey's End would still have its reputation as 'Retirement Living at Its Finest.'"

I had hit a nerve, and for a moment, Davis put his face in his hands and looked down at his desk. I held my breath, hoping he wouldn't cry in my presence.

"This entire episode has been a nightmare," he said, looking up at me with dry eyes. "But it's over, and I do believe everyone here is settling down to their former sense of well-being and safety."

Before leaving his office, I was tempted to give notice of my departure from Journey's End, but didn't want to be premature. In her latest e-mail, Sherry indicated she found a complex of condos I might like, and said I should make a trip down to take a look.

But I wasn't going anywhere until Brennan was locked up in San Quentin, and Sam made his decision about starting up a new business. The Feds still had their day in court, and, according to Sam, it was hard to tell when that might occur.

The Chief of Enforcement for the state Department of Corporations reiterated that it was virtually impossible to track all the illegal investments unless somebody complained.

"You know that seniors are the least likely to consult an attorney or report being bilked, out of shame or lack of resources," he told me when I called.

Of course I knew. It had been told to me numerous times in the past year. But I found comfort in knowing that the man who had caused such financial devastation to so many innocent victims would soon be held accountable for four murders, and, eventually, the fraud.

The U.S. Attorney's office in the Northern District of California had seized every penny from Brennan's bank accounts, along with his other assets--the Lexus, the racehorse at Del Mar, and some real estate he owned. Compensation for his victims' losses would come from these assets and the Civil Restitution Fund for those financially harmed who reported their losses.

Before any of this was accomplished, the final nail in Brennan's coffin would be at his sentencing hearing to be held in a few days. I was amazed at how quickly the time passed. At the end of the trial, I thought the sentencing phase would never arrive.

Chapter 48

Sam and I agreed to meet in the courtroom the day of sentencing when I would give a Victim Impact Statement on behalf of Monique. Jacques was unable to make the trip from Paris, and I considered myself the nearest person to a relative. The proceedings began as anticipated when Judge Hemming asked family or friends to approach the dais and make their statements. Mrs. Ryan spoke first on behalf of Mrs. Wilson.

"My husband and I knew Mr. and Mrs. Wilson for many years, and considered them dear friends. When Mr. Wilson died, we marveled at Shirley's courage, self-reliance and fortitude in carrying out the family business with such success. After all her hard work, we were devastated to learn that a financial advisor whom she professed to trust like a brother had swindled much of her wealth.

"Shirley was ashamed to admit that she'd been taken in by this man, so we couldn't convince her to report his crime to the authorities. But she didn't want to ruin his life.

That was so like Shirley, always thinking about the welfare of someone else. And what were the consequences of her charitable decision? That man sitting in the courtroom, stoic and unfeeling, murdered her. He took away this dignified lady's life in a bunch of bushes.

"We will miss Shirley, but my husband and I are gratified to know this malicious man will never see the light of day."

Judge Hemming thanked her and addressed the court. "Unfortunately, Edith Shaw's relatives could not come over from England, and Doctor Rosenberg's family did not care to participate in this portion of the trial. However, Ms. Lawrence, I understand you have a statement to make on behalf of Monique Marquise, so you may step up."

After the calm delivery by Mrs. Ryan, I knew I could never compete with her composure. Although my statement was prepared and written before coming to court, voicing my feelings about Monique would not be easy.

I took a deep breath and began to speak. Too bad if I lost control. I could still tell the court how Monique's death had inflicted pain on me, Jacques and people who never got the chance to know her.

After taking a deep breath, I began to speak in a soft voice. "Monique's cousin, Jacques, lives in Paris and was unable to be here today. He asked me to convey his sorrow and distress over losing this wonderful woman. So I speak of Monique, not as a blood relative, but as my dearest friend at the Journey's End Retirement Home. She was like a sister to me, and her death has left a huge hole in my life. Because of this self-serving, evil man, the world has lost a lovely, gracious, talented woman who had much to offer."

Overcome with emotion, I couldn't continue with the remaining words of my statement. But turning to leave the dais, I pointed to my one-time Friday night date and said in my loudest voice, "That man deserves nothing less than what he gave Monique Marquise—death."

Tears streamed down my cheeks, and loud sobs came from the very depths of my belly.

Chapter 49

With Victim Impact Statements completed, Judge Hemming looked down from the bench and said, "Mr. Brennan, will you please stand?"

The tall man, who once stood straight as a ramrod, stooped over the table like a comma.

"Please proceed with your allocution before I proceed with sentencing."

"What does that mean?" I whispered to Sam.

"Before the judge announces his sentence, he has to admit to killing the victims. It also gives him an opportunity to show remorse, which may influence whether the judge grants leniency."

Inasmuch as he had already accepted a deal of life in prison, I doubted he would show remorse, and, sure enough, after admitting to his crimes, Brennan had nothing more to offer.

Judge Hemming looked at him in disgust and announced, "Lawrence J. Brennan, I hereby sentence you to prison for the rest of your natural life without the possibility of parole. I have been informed by the United States Attorney General's Office that they will be pleading concurrent sentences for federal charges as well as civil lawsuits on behalf of victims involved in fraud cases pending against you."

With those words, Judge Hemming banged her gavel and left the bench. A silence fell over the courtroom, followed by a babble of voices rising from spectators and reporters.

I watched my old friend being led out of the courtroom by sheriff's deputies, and again went through a range of feelings from satisfaction to sadness. Now that I knew who had committed these murders and why, I was curious as to how he'd actually done his dirty deeds. How did he lure Mrs. Wilson to the promenade, and Mrs. Shaw to the mountain trail? How did he get into Monique's apartment and Dr. Irv into the gym in late evening? These questions preyed on my mind, and someday I would find out.

Leaving the courthouse, Sam and I walked to a nearby Italian restaurant. We ordered lunch, although I wasn't hungry. Picking at a chicken salad while Sam devoured a huge plate of linguine and clams, for the first time in my life I found it hard to talk.

"I am so relieved this ordeal is over," I finally said, pushing away my salad. "Can you believe this is the end of a nightmare for so may people?"

"They all end. It's just a question of who wins. Fortunately, this ended with justice on its side in a fairly short time. It doesn't always happen that way. Look at Rebecca's killing, and how long it took for that horror to be resolved. Too bad Jose and Pablo can't share a cell with Brennan at Quentin."

"Don't felons, like these three, get separate cells?"

"Of course. I was trying to lighten things up, because you look like you just lost your best friend."

"In some perverted way, I did. Any idea when he will he be transferred to San Quentin from the county jail?'

"As soon as they get him processed. Could take a week, maybe more. Why? You're not thinking of visiting this creep again, are you?"

"Maybe. I want to find out how he lured these people to the places where he killed them."

"Lily, leave it alone. He's going to pay for the rest of his life. Not only for the murders, but his financial schemes. So let it be."

"I can't. I have to know how he persuaded these residents to go somewhere where he could murder them."

My opportunity to get an answer to that question came a few days later when I reported to Joan for my volunteer job. She invited me to lunch in the County cafeteria, curious as to how I was holding up since the trial ended.

I told her what I told Sam. There were questions remaining, and the only way to get answers was to go to the source.

"Joan, could you arrange a visit for me with Brennan in San Quentin?"

"I'll talk to Joe and see what we can do."

Chapter 50

I wasn't sure if seeing my old friend behind bars a second time was a great idea. Following the first visit, I'd come away angry at his arrogance and lack of repentance. Would he be a different man after pleading guilty to the murders and being sentenced to life in prison? I wondered how he was dealing with the reality of a lifetime of incarceration for the murders, not to mention the additional years for robbing the elderly of their savings? Was he feeling remorse? Did he realize he would die in jail an old, broken man? There was one bright note in his future at Quentin. His lack of sexual appeal would place him low on the list for the most desperate, deranged deviants.

After receiving permission to visit Brennan, I was determined to find out every detail omitted from the trial. Driving to its gates, I remembered being to the penitentiary years before when the State allowed tours. But my only recollection of its interior was the green-painted room with one piece of furniture in the middle. It was the execution chamber, and the electric chair was still in use. Visiting the prison again was not something I looked forward to, but if I was to know the entire story of the murders, I had to hear it from the killer himself.

After parking the Mini, I sat and stared at the ominous building sitting on one of the most beautiful sites in Northern California, the San Francisco Bay. Sprawling over 400 acres, at last count, it was home to over 6,000 inmates. Recently, there were proposals in the state legislature to close it or move it, but it still stood on the bay front as it has since its opening in 1852.

As one state assemblyman once said, "The main footprint of San Quentin is likely a permanent fixture here in Marin," adding that, "the wasteful and unnecessary death row expansion must be stopped in favor of creating a transit village that could include housing for working families, limited commercial space, and offices for non-profit organizations that serve inmates."

At the time, I thought his proposal a very good idea, but not being a member of the California State Assembly made my agreement a moot point. Passing through several doors to enter the main building, I head loud clicks as they closed behind me. Nearing the interior, I began to hear shouting, blaring televisions, and loud banging sounds that seemed to flood the cavernous space.

After having my purse searched, I walked through a

narrow entry, and was escorted by a large Hispanic guard down a bleak cement hallway. It was twenty minutes before Lawrence Brennan hobbled into the visitor area in wrist-to-leg shackles. He was cuffed to the table as the guard watched over us from the other side of a large wired-glass window.

"Thank you, Lily, for visiting when you have every right to never want to see my face again."

I was surprised at his words, considering he knew I was the person responsible for his being here. Looking at him closely, I could see he'd lost a lot of weight in only a month. From what I heard about prison food, he would most likely gain back the lost pounds after a few more weeks.

"I'm not interested in seeing you. I'm here because I need some answers."

"You should have all the answers you want after testifying against me, and being in court every day."

His words stung, because they were said with sadness, not anger.

"I know why you killed those four innocent people, but I need to know how you lured them to their deaths."

There was a long stretch of silence, reminding me of our Friday night dinners when I would fill empty spaces of quiet with chatter about my life. Now, in retrospect, I realized that by talking about his past, he risked losing his future.

"I have nothing more to lose now, so I'll tell you anything you want to know, including things you may not want to hear.

"That year we had dinner on Friday nights meant a lot to me, Lily, and not because it was a break from Journey's End food. I was attracted to you, wanted to spend time with you, loved hearing stories from your past. You were a breath of fresh air in my stifling world. But with a criminal past hanging over me, I could never have let you know my feelings."

Always suspecting he cared about me in some strange way, I wasn't shocked by his words; only grateful he'd never expressed them as a free man. It was his lack of attachment and mysterious aloofness that kept me interested.

"But that's not what you wanted to hear, is it? You want me to give you details of the killings."

"Yes. And start from the beginning."

"Shirley Wilson was the first to approach me demanding I repay the money she lost in our dealings. She threatened to tell everyone at Journey's End that I was a thief, and said she would go to the authorities if I didn't come up with her $600,000 nest egg. I didn't have the money, and couldn't have her going to the police.

"The day before you found her on the promenade, I'd convinced her to accept $300,000 as a down payment and another $300,000 the following week. She agreed to let me wheel her to the promenade the next morning so I could pay her without being seen. And you know how the morning ended."

After taking a deep breath, he went on. "I didn't know if I could really do it or how I'd feel after the fact. I was surprised when I didn't feel relief or guilt. Her killing was easier than I expected, and when it was over, I felt nothing.

"I did feel sorrow over Edna Shaw. She was a sweet little Brit, but on the day of the picnic, she confronted me about the $240,000 she'd lost on an annuity I'd sold her. I said we had to discuss the problem in private and suggested we find a trail away from the crowd. I pushed her wheelchair up a road until it ended with a ravine. Without any planning, I just shoved her chair into the gully and watched it roll over and over. It was a risky thing to do at a picnic with so many people around, but after getting away with killing Mrs. Wilson, I knew there was no limit to what I could do."

Realizing I was in the presence of a psychopath, I braced myself for what he'd done to Monique. Proud and private, Monique never told me she'd been bilked of money. Always putting on a happy, bright face, it wasn't in her nature to talk of anything negative. Hell, I didn't even know about her ex-husband, even though I'd told her everything about my three.

"Now, Monique was classy enough to invite me to her apartment to discuss our unfortunate financial dealings.

She said going to the authorities was the last thing she wanted to do, but she was stretched for money. Without the extra income she expected from the real estate deal I'd sold her, she didn't know if she was able to continue living at Journey's End. She told me she was going to talk to Dr. Irv about the situation first, as he was a smart man who could give her some advice. That's when I realized I had two complications to deal with.

"Getting rid of Monique took little thought when I noticed the scarf around her neck. All it took was a strong tug until she stopped breathing. To make it look like an accident, I took the end of the scarf and wrapped it around the front wheel."

Imagining Monique's fear and pain, I felt nauseous and woozy. But I swallowed the bile gathering in my mouth, and tried to hang on for a little while longer.

"Of course, I had to take care of Dr. Irv right away, but he was easy. Frail man, that old doc, and too trusting, because I had no trouble commandeering his scooter after dinner one night and suggesting we go to the gym. I knew he liked the recumbent machine, so I told him a new one was installed that day and asked if he would like to take a look. Once there, I pretended to help him onto the machine, and let his head slip. That was all it took to finish the old man. After Dr. Irv, I thought my problems were solved until you, my dear Lily, got nosy and stirred up the hornet's nest. Are you satisfied with the outcome of your work?"

"I would be more satisfied if I saw you strapped on a gurney with a needle in your arm."

Chapter 51

After my disturbing encounter with Brennan, I drove to the beach and sat on a bench watching the sea ebb in and out. I took deep breaths, trying to feel one with nature as I'd been taught in yoga, but I was a poor student. My mind flew here and there like the seagulls chattering above me.

The smell of sea air and the warmth of the sun reminded me of Cabo San Lucas. I thought about that week a lot lately, remembering the feelings of satisfaction and happiness I felt when it was over. Sure, the beauty of the place had something to do with my feeling of contentment, but it was only a background to the day in my hotel room when Jose sold Sam his menorah.

Something told me finding Jose at the Lizard Lounge wasn't mere coincidence. It was Sam's investigative skills. And identifying the Journey's End killer was more than pure luck. Yes, I worked my ass off searching the computer and prying around, but using the instincts I learned from Sam played a big part. Because we still had the touch, Jose, Pablo and Brennan languished in prison where they would be until their dying days.

What had brought me to progress and peace these last two years? I studied the gray fog drifting across the sand and thought about discovering the truth behind Lloyd Bellingham's facade and the capture of Jose. On both occasions, my feelings were the most profound I'd experienced in a very long time. I saw that in Sam's demeanor, too, after the capture of Rebecca's killer. Putting bad guys away felt almost as good as my vague recollection of a great orgasm.

With everything going on, I hadn't reminded Sam of my idea, but I knew life would be empty if I sat around doing nothing. I didn't know if two old farts could make a difference, but saving some helpless victim caught in a financial scam might save one person from devastation. Many investors lacked resources to research an advisor, and what options did they have? If my newly devised plan worked, maybe Sam and I could help these potential victims. We would charge them nothing to investigate a potential investment and the company selling it. The business would be advertised as a non-profit for the elderly.

I hurried to Rosie, suddenly eager to get an answer from

Sam on my idea. His machine answered. "Leave a message and phone number. I'll get back to you upon my return home."

"Sam, I need to talk to you immediately, so call me as soon as you get in. As a matter of fact, come for dinner tomorrow night. Lamb curry is on the menu, and I know you enjoyed it last time."

He apparently did enjoy the curry, because within the next hour, Sam was on the phone, saying he would love to come for dinner. We met in the lobby the next night, and went to the dining room where we found a table for two. I recounted my last visit to the jail, and the sordid details I was told of the killings.

"Without any emotion, Brennan related in detail, the manner in which he lured each of his victims to their death. I hate to admit it, Sam, but I'm sure the man is a psychopath."

"Are you surprised? Most serial killers are generally sick in the head."

"I suppose that's true, but I once thought this particular psycho was a thoughtful, kind man. Maybe that makes me sick in the head, too. It's really hard to believe he's not only a killer, but also a thief who stole money from the elderly."

I had planned to segue into the conversation I wanted to discuss.

Sam wasn't a greedy man or one who needed life's

luxury, but the idea of giving away his talent might strike him as unimaginable, so I had to appeal to his soft heart.

"Have you thought about my plan?"

"A little."

"And have you thought about these elderly people, most of them smart in many ways, who are being bilked out of their hard-earned money? They're helpless victims. As you told me, financial abuse of the elderly is a serious and common crime. And if someone is low-income, they are the least likely to consult an attorney."

"We're not attorneys, Lily."

"I know, but we could help prevent these people from needing an attorney by checking financial advisors for authenticity. You know, the ones who advertise, 'Come to a free estate-planning seminar. Learn how to save money and plan for long term care.'"

"And how do you propose we do that?"

"We start a non-profit business using our know-how and suspicious personalities. You are already licensed, so we contact the Secretary of State to file paperwork for registering our business name, remember Levine & Lawrence, Private Investigators. Giving people financial guidance will give us both purpose in our twilight years."

"And where do you plan to run this business—your apartment at the Home?'

"I decided months ago, I'll be leaving Journey's End

soon. I thought of buying a condo in Southern California, but if we start the business, I'll look at housing in Oakland. Maybe near your place. We can run the business from one of our condos, saving us the overhead of office space.

"We'll advertise on the Internet with a Web site, and I can make visits to retirement homes and places where the elderly congregate, telling them of our services. Like I did on the Brennan case, we'll use the Internet for background checking. I have a computer and printer. You have locking file cabinets and other PI paraphernalia we might need.

"What do you think, Sam?"

"This is a lot to digest, my friend. You know I've been semi-retired, and don't know if I want to take on something that sounds like a full-time job."

"I understand you need time to mull it over, but while you contemplate your navel, old people are being scammed."

Laying on a guilt trip always worked for my mother, so maybe it would work for me.

We left the dining room, and Sam left me in the lobby. He planted a kiss on my cheek, and said he'd call in a day or two.

Chapter 52

Knowing Sam's Jewish guilt equaled my Catholic guilt, there was no question he would find my altruistic idea something to be considered. And, sure enough, several days after our talk over lamb curry, Sam called.

"If I agree to go along with this PI business in which we'll make no money, take only clients who are old and maybe financially destitute, do I at least get to run the show?"

"Of course. Haven't you always run the show? Besides, I'll be busy finding us clients."

And that was the beginning of Levine & Lawrence, Private Investigating. I called Sherry to tell her of my change of plans, as I was staying in the Bay Area, and began my search for a condo near Sam.

"Will it bother you if I find something near your place?"

"No problem. Actually, it will be good for running the business. And, hey, I may even take you to dinner on

Friday night every so often so you don't miss Lloyd or living at the Home."

"Sometimes you have a very sick sense of humor."

Actually, I was thrilled at the thought of having a man to socialize with now and then.

Sam lived in a lovely area near a vibrant waterfront, so I started looking in his complex. As luck would have it, there were two very nice units available in my price range. We decided that since Sam had the license, extra room, file cabinets and PI equipment, the office would be at his place. I purchased a small unit two floors below Sam's where I would keep the computer and printer.

When escrow closed on my condo, I called Dick Davis and asked when he was available for a chat. We'd been on friendlier terms since the trial, when Dicky realized I wasn't quite the nut case he'd always assumed.

"I'm free right now, Lily, if you want to come down."

Within five minutes I was seated in his office, telling him I would be leaving Journey's End in sixty days. Never before had an encounter with Dicky been so satisfying. I told him I was moving to a condo in Oakland, but had no reason to tell him of my new venture with Sam. I assumed that after leaving the Home no one would give a damn about Lily Lawrence, and I would, hopefully, be forgotten. All that mattered to me now was that I felt like a new woman, one who could tackle anything in the future. What was that old saying? *Freedom is like taking a bath—you have to keep doing it every day!*

Davis expressed words of regret—most likely because he had another vacancy to fill—but we shook hands, and I made an insincere comment about staying in touch. I needed sixty days to prepare the new condo with a few upgrades, and put my finances in order. Except for Roy, who was devastated by my news, there was no one at Journey's End I would miss.

After many trips to Oakland, checking on contractors working on my new home, I was ready for a final ride across the bridge. It was a spring afternoon. The miniscule trunk of the Mini was loaded with clothes, important papers, and a few valuables that I didn't trust to the moving van. After backing my car from the middle of garbage bins, I pressed a buzzer to open the security gates and drove down the hill.

The sun was shining, the sky was blue, traffic was light, and I was leaving Journey's End for the last time. A new business venture lay ahead—one I considered my purpose in life—making progress and finding peace.

Epilogue

Chapter 53

Not long after marketing our venture as FREE FINANCIAL INVESTIGATING FOR THE ELDERLY, Levine & Lawrence, Private Investigators, was teeming with clients. When he was in a curmudgeon mood, I'd sometimes hear Sam mutter, "Oy vey, the money we could be raking in if this business was for profit."

But the times of greatest satisfaction, overriding the desire to make money, were the occasions we helped the elderly, and, sometimes, not so elderly clients, avoid a particularly heinous scam. If the mantra for buying real estate is Location, Location, Location, we discovered our business success was the result of Timing, Timing, Timing.

The Obama Health Care Initiative, recently launched, presented another avenue for scam artists to ply their trade. A confused population of Medicare patients was being scared shitless about losing their healthcare, making them easy targets for unsolicited phone calls from "insurance experts" requesting all manner of private information. After getting word of this new fraud, Sam and I launched an informational seminar at various senior facilities to provide the uninformed with the true facts.

Meanwhile, these unsavory advisors were prowling for prey by advertising expertise on living trusts, annuities, or estate planning. The come-ons arrived in the form of mail, telephone calls, door-to-door solicitations, even phony doctors. Aware of the pitfalls in this type of tactic, some of the intended targets came to us for assistance. Investigating the shysters resulted in our spending many hours verifying outlandish claims.

We also became an unofficial clearinghouse for seniors facing minor exploitations—the ubiquitous vacuum cleaner salesman, hidden bank fees, unauthorized purchases on credit cards, sale of expired "coupons." The list went on. In most cases, we acted as a scary go-between for the elderly and rip-off artist, but if the case looked too extreme, or was ripe for an attorney, Sam's Rolodex was filled with names of lawyers. Sometimes, our advice was simply "Buyer Beware."

The gratitude from our non-paying clients came in the form of fruit baskets, bags of homegrown vegetables, casseroles and, sometimes, unidentifiable food items. They filled our condos, and eventually Sam and I began to share our bounty at dinner. Usually, we ate at his condo. He had a real dining area; I had a kitchen bar with two stools.

And, once a week, on Friday night, we dined at one of the many fine restaurants in our neighborhood. What started as a joke and reminder of Lawrence Brennan soon became the highlight of our workweek.

I refused to go out in public until he got rid of the fedora. "You have the menorah as a memento of your wedding to Rebecca, so don't you think it's time to get rid of the hat?"

Soon after, I saw it on the head of the maintenance man at our condo complex. Surprised he readily agreed, I began to see Sam in an entirely different light. I found myself attracted to his head of wavy gray hair and vibrant blue eyes but, more than his newly noted physical assets, my heart warmed when I saw his compassion and eagerness when helping people who came to us for advice.

He stopped calling me "big sister" when we started Levine & Lawrence, telling me it sounded unprofessional, but I sensed he, too, saw our relationship as more than business partner and friend. I kept my feelings in check because I struggled with the stigma of our May-December ages. Not because of the five years between us, but because he was the May and I was December. I never dreamed in my seventies I could be classified as a "cougar."

Sometimes, I enumerated other reasons I should continue to think of Sam as my boss—the man I worked for these many years. I used his Jewishness and my Catholicism as a roadblock, when in actuality neither of us had practiced our religions since childhood. That obstacle was eliminated quickly.

Since my last husband's death, I swore a romantic relationship was not in my future, and planned to remain single until my dying day. Life was good. I had my own condo, freedom, and peace. Then, before I could control the force predetermining my destiny, fate stepped in on a Friday night over petrale sole at the Jack London Bar & Grill.

After pushing his plate away and taking a huge gulp of his Sauvignon Blanc, Sam looked across the table at me. There was softness in his eyes I hadn't seen since Rebecca left his life many years before.

"You know, Lily, we make one helluva team, and I've been thinking about us a lot lately. We're not getting any younger. We share a business, most meals, and we're together almost 24/7. It seems to me our lives would make a lot more sense if we teamed up in a more personal way. What do you think about growing older together as man and wife?"

It wasn't the most romantic proposal I'd heard in my seventy years, and it was the first marriage proposal I'd been presented before a first kiss, but I was sure the kiss was imminent. Deeply touched, I found myself reaching for his hand.

"You know, Sam, I've been having the same thoughts. If I must grow older, you are the only one I want to share the experience. Just promise we'll never move to another version of Journey's End.

Lightning Source UK Ltd.
Milton Keynes UK
UKOW02f0618140815

256928UK00003B/97/P

9 781304 450692